PEARL OF THE ORIENT

Full Page of Moon Photos
Los Angeles Times
FINAL
The Globe and Mail
Diplomat kills fighter
VIET CRISIS GROWS
Viet Cong suicide mission
wiped out at U.S. Embassy
Dies In Viet
Parts of building
held for 6 hours
1st Photos of Viet Mass
SUICIDE RAID ON
THE EMBASSY
LIFE
THE PLAIN DEALER
Chicago Tribune
RECAPTURE U.S. EMBASSY
GIs Land in Copters on Saigon Roof,
Wipe Out Viet Cong in 6-Hour Battle
The New York Times
VC HIT SAIGON
Vietnam Casualt
Reds Invade Embassy, Air Base
XTRA
Los Angeles Times
FINAL
STAR   RIPES

PEARL OF THE ORIENT

an original screenplay
by

Bart Marshall

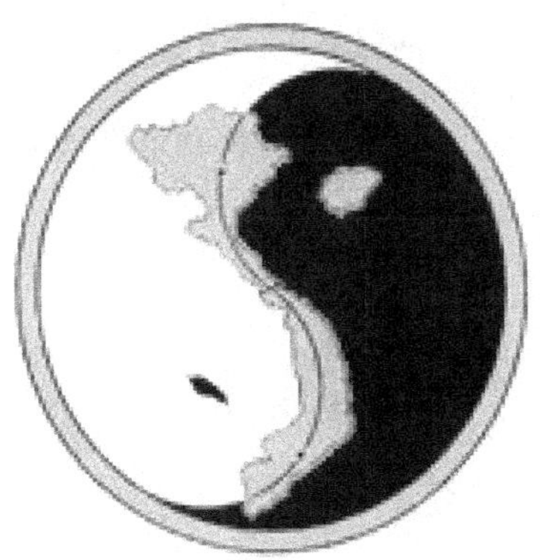

REALFACE PRESS

Published by Realface Press
info@realface.com

ISBN: 978-0-9992583-0-9

Also published by Realface Press:

Christ Sutras*: The Complete Sayings of Jesus
from All Sources Arranged into Sermons,*
compiled and composed by Bart Marshall

The Perennial Way*, Extended Edition,*
translated by Bart Marshall

Bhagavad Gita*: The Definitive Translation,*
translated by Bart Marshall

The Triune Self*: Confessions of a Ruthless Seer,*
by Mike Snider

The Conquest of Illusion*, by J.J. van der Leeuw,
90th Anniversary Edition, edited by Bart Marshall

Letters of Transmission*: The Enlightenment Method of
Zen Master Alfred Pulyan,* edited by Bart Marshall

After the Absolute*, by David Gold with Bart Marshall

Think and Grow Rich*, by Napoleon Hill,
80th Anniversary Edition, edited by Bart Marshall

Magic, White and Black*, by Franz Hartmann, M.D.,
edited by Bart Marshall

The Torah*: The Five Books of Moses,
King James Readers' Version,* by Bart Marshall

Verses Regarding True Nature*, by Bart Marshall

Introduction

Pearl of the Orient is an unproduced screenplay inspired by a true story—highly dramatized and hyperbolized, of course. It had a shot at Hollywood a number of years ago, being passed on by name-brand directors and such, and since has been collecting dust in the virtual bottom drawer of my laptop. Recently, in a moment of nostalgia for Vietnam, I pulled it up, reread it, and still liked it—a lot.

I realized, though, that I bring to my reading of it a huge amount of background and imagery that is not on the page, and began giving serious consideration to making the movie myself, even planning a trip to Vietnam to scout locations and talk with a production company I found there. Through a series of mistakes on my part, and cosmic intervention, that trip did not happen.

In the aftermath, I had a "What was I thinking?" moment. At age 72 with no prior experience directing films, just who did I think would finance me? My flight of fancy was fun while it lasted, and to be honest, mixed with my disappointment was great relief. A burden had been lifted. For decades I had felt like I had a "responsibility" to create some kind of art from what was a unique and compelling experience of the Vietnam War. When my "heroic" effort to do it all myself fell through, that all went away.

What I decided, though, was to create an artifact of that obsession, something I could hold in my hand. Hence, this book. It is the screenplay slightly rewritten into what I hope is a more readable format than a shooting script, sort of a cross between a screenplay and a novella. It is all I need to feel done and complete with this story.

However, if this book should find its way into the hands of someone who somehow sees what I see in it, and would like to put it on the screen, please let me know. Hope springs eternal, and all that.

Bart Marshall
marshallbart@gmail.com

Suong Le

PEARL OF THE ORIENT

A Film in Five Acts

Randy Noone

FADE IN

<u>PROLOGUE</u>: IN A BUDDHIST TEMPLE IN VIETNAM

An OLD MONK hovers over a table, his calligraphy brush poised above a MAP of Southeast Asia.

SUPER: "VIETNAM, 1963"

His brush delicately outlines North and South Vietnam, and with a brief stroke, the DMZ that divides them.

FLASH CUT: EXTREME CLOSE-UP OF FLAMES

The monk continues to ink his brush and draw.

BEGIN CREDITS

He places a dot in the center of Hanoi, a dot in the center of Saigon. He outlines *Hi Nam* Island in the South China Sea, then colors in *Ton Le Sap* Lake in Cambodia.

FLASH CUT: EXTREME CLOSE-UP OF FLAMES

He draws a graceful "S" that swoops the exact middle of the two countries — the apogee of the northern curve intersecting the center of Hanoi, the apogee of the southern, Saigon. The center of the "S" splits the DMZ exactly.

FLASH CUT: EXTREME CLOSE-UP OF FLAMES

He encloses it all in a flawless circle, completing a YIN-YANG SYMBOL in perfect attunement with the geography of Vietnam.

IN A CITY IN VIETNAM

A black MERCEDES creeps down a narrow street crowded with scooters, cyclos, bicycles, pedestrians.

IN THE CAR a well-heeled, harshly beautiful Vietnamese woman rides regally in back. She is MADAME YEN, thirties.

OUTSIDE AN ORPHANAGE IN VIETNAM

The Mercedes arrives. The DRIVER, a Vietnamese man with an aura of the underworld, steps around to open the rear door. Madame Yen gracefully emerges. The driver bows.

                           DRIVER
          Madame Yen...

IN THE ORPHANAGE a Vietnamese Catholic NUN leads Madame Yen past the many CHILDREN. The faint sound of Billie Holliday SINGING the opening lines of "God Bless the Child" can be heard.

A YOUNG GIRL mouths the words so perfectly she appears to be the source of the song. Off in her own world, she sings softly, gesturing as if on stage. She is TRINH SUONG LE, 13, a child on the cusp of sensuality. Around her neck, a black velvet choker with cameo.

Madame Yen stops in front of her. Startled, Suong Le quickly lifts the tone arm, scratching the record. The last words heard are, "Papa may have, but—"

Madame Yen looks her over in silence. Behind Suong Le, a crucifix hangs above her bed. On a small table, a photograph of her dead parents holding an infant.

Madame Yen hands the nun a wad of MONEY. The nun bows. Madame Yen extends a jeweled hand to Suong Le.

IN A CITY IN VIETNAM

An old WHITE SEDAN crawls up a narrow crowded street. The driver is a young monk with glasses. The OLD MONK who drew the yin-yang symbol sits in the back. Next to him is DAO, a middle-aged monk with an interesting, distinctive face.

A black MERCEDES slowly approaches from the other direction, down the same narrow street.

IN THE MERCEDES Madame Yen and Suong Le ride in back. Madame Yen touches Suong Le's hair in a manner more intimate than motherly. Suong Le turns away and looks out her window.

SUONG LE watches the white sedan creep slowly past, not two feet away. Dao smiles at her and nods a polite bow.

DAO watches as Suong Le returns his smile.

OVERHEAD SHOT of the black and white cars slowly passing.

SUONG LE continues to look at Dao for as long as she can, as if he might somehow save her.

END CREDITS

AT A BUSY CITY INTERSECTION

The WHITE SEDAN stops and the driver raises the hood. The OLD MONK and DAO walk to the enter of the intersection. Dao carries a gasoline can. The old monk sits lotus position in the street. A large group of Buddhists wait reverently. Traffic stops, onlookers gather.

Dao places the gasoline can next to the old monk and steps back. His expression is complex as he bows to his friend and spiritual master for the last time.

The old monk raises the gasoline can above his head and pours the entire contents over himself. He serenely sets the can aside, and for several moments sits motionless.

A WESTERN MAN wearing a photographer's vest looks on in disbelief, then quickly raises a professional CAMERA.

From the folds of the old monk's robe a LIGHTER appears. The SOUND of it opening is bell clear.

THE OLD MONK'S FACE is impassive. In silence, the SOUND of the lighter wheel is deafening. His face becomes FIRE.

PULL BACK to full shot of the BURNING MONK, a dark silhouette engulfed in flames—a BUDDHA STATUE against a background of RAGING ORANGE. Soft flickering SOUND OF FLAMES...

ACT I: IN THE CENTRAL HIGHLANDS OF VIETNAM

We take a long silent look at a vast primeval landscape of abrupt jungle peaks shrouded in mist...

SUPER: "VIETNAM, 1967— FOUR YEARS LATER"

In the distance, two HUEY HELICOPTERS silently enter frame like dark prehistoric birds.

SHOCK CUT: OPEN DOOR OF HUEY as the SUDDEN LOUD SOUND of chopper blades makes the heart skip.

In the door sits Staff Sergeant RANDY NOONE, tiger fatigues, bush hat, combat gear. Twenties, good-looking, intelligent—a guy who could write his own ticket in life. Yet here he is, perched on the edge, legs dangling in nothing.

Behind him sit five HMONG STRIKERS, equipped as he is. Noone's hands press the floor as if ready to push off.

NOONE'S P.O.V. as he looks past his boots to the jungle below.

NOONE pushes off into a slow motion FREE FALL, spread-eagle on his back looking up at the sky. His face beams JOY...

THE DOORGUNNER of Noone's chopper has a brief conversation into his headset, then turns to Noone—who still sits beside him—and thumbs a high-sign. Noone shakes himself out of his REVERIE and yells to his strikers.

NOONE

    Get ready!

He looks across to the OTHER HUEY flying a short distance away, also full of Hmong strikers.

In the door sits Sergeant First Class LYLE DECKER, a tattooed Special Forces lifer prone to bar fights. He flips Noone a casual bird—for luck.

Noone flips one back. The blades beat tense rhythm. It is the moment of waiting for the moment...

Suddenly, the choppers drop in a breathtaking descent to treetop level, then skim it in an EXHILARATING RIDE through steep jungle canyons.

NOONE'S P.O.V. as the trees fly by just under his dangling boots.

THE CHOPPERS drop into a small clearing. The PATROL runs for the tree line, leaves and branches slapping, then hits the ground. The sound of choppers fades to silence. The sound of INSECTS fades up.

                    DECKER
          Let's go.

The patrol moves through triple-canopy jungle. Snakes, monkeys, colorful birds, the barely-detectable face of a TIGER. At overlooks great vistas unfold of mist-clouded peaks — haunting and mysterious.

THAT EVENING Noone reclines against his rucksack, sweat-soaked shirt open to the waist, working with compass and map.

DECKER sits nearby, shirtless. Among his tattoos is a NECKLACE OF DASHES and the words, "Cut on dotted line."

                    NOONE
          Amazing how much of these mountains are still
          un-mapped.

His MAP shows a large amoeba-like blob of white in the midst of an otherwise detailed topography.

                    NOONE
          We're three clicks into nowhere. Feels different
          in a white hole.

Decker lights a smoke.

                    DECKER
          Mountains are mountains.

                    NOONE
Like maybe the rules of the universe don't mean
shit here.

                    DECKER
Jungle's jungle.

                    NOONE
Gives the operation an edge.

                    DECKER
Snatches got enough edge by themselves.

BAAP CANH, Hmong, forties, hands Noone a canteen cup of hot
water. Noone pours it into a plastic bag of rations and stirs.

                    BAAP CANH
Poncho.

Noone leans forward. Baap Canh takes a poncho from his rucksack.

                    DECKER
You ain't said dick about your extension leave.

                    NOONE
It was all right. Stayed with some friends.

                    DECKER
What about your parents?

                    NOONE
Not a place I want to be.

                    DECKER
Yeah, mansions are hell.

                    NOONE
Nothing's what it seems.

                    DECKER
It is what it is.

                              NOONE
          Can't argue with that.

BAAP CANH strings up a poncho, along with REEBY, Noone's
young Hmong radioman. They lay another poncho on the ground
beneath it, and a third for their blanket. The three of them are
inseparable on operation.

                              DECKER
          This is my last one for awhile. Cobb's pulling
          me in on an Agency thing. Came up while you
          were gone.

                              NOONE
          What kind of thing?

                              DECKER
          Something with FULRO. Working for a guy
          named Jakes.

                              NOONE
          Carter Jakes?

                              DECKER
          Know him?

                              NOONE
          Heard his name a lot at Intel School. Kennedy's
          man inside the coup. What's he up to now?

                              DECKER
          More of the same you might say.

                              NOONE
          Meaning what?

                              DECKER
          Hush-hush, top secret—

                              NOONE
          Fuck you—

                              DECKER
                  Eyes only, need to know.

                              NOONE
                  Any spots open or is it for old fucks only?

                              DECKER
                  It's for ass-kicking motherfuckers, that's who.

                              NOONE
                  Seriously.

                              DECKER
                  Seriously what?

                              NOONE
                  Asshole.

Decker blows smoke rings.

                              DECKER
                  I already put the word in for you with Cobb.
                  Not that you fucking need it. Somehow he's got
                  the mistaken idea your shit don't stink.

                              NOONE
                  Thanks.

                              DECKER
                  Self-preservation. I've gotten kinda used to you
                  watching my back.

                              NOONE
                        (shared moment)
                  Same here.

IN AN APARTMENT IN VIETNAM

CIA officer CARTER JAKES, forties, stands at a dark window, staring
into the night. There's a KNOCK.

                            JAKES
          It's open.

Master Sergeant FRANK COBB, forties, strides in. Weathered face,
faded fatigues, wrist full of Montagnard bracelets. He has an
intimidating presence unrelated to size.

                            JAKES
          Where's Decker? We need more muscle for this
          kind of shit.

                            COBB
          Got tapped for one more op.

                            JAKES
          I thought you had it handled.

                            COBB
          So did I. It's handled now.

Jakes pockets a 9mm.
                            JAKES
          This is no way to run a revolution.

                            COBB
          It's just a snatch. We'll have him full time in a
          few days.

                            JAKES
          I don't trust Tong not to do something stupid.

                            COBB
          So why agree to meet like this? We don't need
          him.

                            JAKES
          Not at the moment. Things change.

Jakes jams a second gun into his back waistband and drops his shirt
over it.

                              JAKES
          Let's go.

ON WATERFRONT DOCKS IN VIETNAM AT NIGHT

JAKES and COBB pull up in a jeep. Cobb grabs an M-16 as they head
for the door of a warehouse.

INSIDE THE WAREHOUSE they look around in dim light. Shadows
protrude at odd angles. From nowhere, four Vietnamese GOONS
appear.

                              GOON 1
          General say no guns.

He reaches for Cobb's M-16. Cobb jams it into his chest.

                              COBB
          That ain't gonna happen.

The other goons pull .45s. A 9mm appears in Jake's hand.

                              JAKES
          No sense being pricks about this.

                              GENERAL TONG (O.S.)
          It's all right. Mister Jakes and I are old friends.

GENERAL TONG, fifties, oily, vague aura of sadistic homosexuality,
emerges from shadow in a dark suit.

                              JAKES
          General.

                              GENERAL TONG
                       (offering Jakes a cigar)
          Cuban?

Jakes takes it and puts it in his pocket. Tong smiles at the insult and
puts one between his thin lips. A goon flicks a lighter. Tong takes his
time. His face holds fierce shadows.

                          JAKES
Your meeting.

                      GENERAL TONG
Those sexy black airplanes of yours have been
transporting quite a lot of opium lately.

                          JAKES
Not nearly as much as your Air Force.

                      GENERAL TONG
But the tribes seem to prefer doing business
with you — now that they have a choice.

                          JAKES
We help a few strategic villages get their crops
to market. Build alliances.

                      GENERAL TONG
Last month you transported three times as much
as the previous month.

                          JAKES
Hearts and minds...

                      GENERAL TONG
If you sold to me there would be no problem.

                          JAKES
I have a commitment to honor.

                      GENERAL TONG
Honor. Yes...
                (puffs cigar)
I'll pay fifty percent more than you're getting
from her.

                          JAKES
Very generous, but as I said —

GENERAL TONG
Madame Yen is a relic of the past. She cannot
compete with me.

JAKES
And yet, here we are.

GENERAL TONG
I will soon control the entire market, with or
without you.

JAKES
Should that happen, I'll sell to you.

GENERAL TONG
I may not feel so generous then.

JAKES
I'll take my chances.

Tong dips his head in the slightest of bows, then ponders his cigar
with philosophical menace.

GENERAL TONG
The memory of a woman's intimate scent... How
many unfortunate decisions in history have
resulted from no more than this?

IN THE NIGHT JUNGLE MOUNTAINS

NOONE reclines against his rucksack, smoking a Camel. BAAP
CANH squats on his heels nearby, smoking a small pipe. He has a
likable Yoda-esque quality. They talk softly as old friends in both
English and Rhade.

NOONE
You go on operation while I was gone?

BAAP CANH
Everyone but you think I too old for bodyguard.

                    NOONE
          You are, but you make good coffee.

Baap Canh puffs his pipe.

                    BAAP CANH
          You like being in America?

                    NOONE
          Sometimes.

                    BAAP CANH
          You like Vietnam more?

                    NOONE
          Sometimes.

                    BAAP CANH
          You are like me. Nowhere is home.

                    NOONE
          You were a village shaman...

                    BAAP CANH
          A village is not home. I am called Baap Canh
          "No-Village."

                    NOONE
                (laughs)
          I love it.

They smoke in silence.

                    NOONE
          What would a shaman have to tell me
          if I asked?

Baap Canh regards him a moment, then intones a soft chant.

                                BAAP CANH
                          (in Rhade, subtitles)
                     Fear nothing, do not flee...
                     Eat the pig within...
                     Eat the monkey within...
                     Drink the rice wine within...

Noone listens.

                                BAAP CANH
                     Do not seek the soup of another...
                     Do not seek the rice of another...
                     Do not seek the house of another.

THE NEXT DAY IN THE JUNGLE

Shards of sunlight angle down as if into a cathedral. The patrol
moves cautiously through lush foliage then stops. NOONE glides up
to DECKER and whispers.

                                  NOONE
                     We gotta be close.

                                  DECKER
                     They'll have ambushes all in here.

The patrol moves with great stealth, using only hand signals,
stopping occasionally to listen. They hear something. It's the
incongruous whine of a TRUCK.

ON THE HO CHI MINH TRAIL a North Vietnamese Army (NVA)
truck bumps along carrying NVA soldiers, rifles bristling. More
soldiers follow on foot.

NOONE and DECKER creep forward and watch them pass.

                                  DECKER
                     Go north a ways. Let me know when a
                     straggler's coming. I'll set up the snatch here.

Noone motions to Baap Canh, Reeby, and TRANH, a tough-looking
Hmong striker. They move to a position further north on the trail.

14

DECKER watches and waits.

NOONE watches and waits. Finally, the faint sound of engines.

ON THE TRAIL a large convoy of trucks and troops approaches.

INSIDE A TRUCK CAB rides COLONEL HAN, forties, a poet-warrior. He looks uncomfortable. He clutches a roll of toilet paper. [*NVA dialogue is in Vietnamese with subtitles.*]

> COLONEL HAN
> Stop.

His driver speaks into a radio handset and hits the brakes.

NOONE watches the convoy stop and sees Colonel Han hurry into the jungle — straight for him!

> NOONE
> (bare whisper)
> Holy shit!

COLONEL HAN stops, turns his back to the unseen Noone and drops his pants. His face shows relief. He glances casually to his left and sees Tranh, trying his best to look invisible. Tranh smiles.

Han opens his mouth just as Noone's hand slams over it. Instantly he is thrown to the ground, Noone's knife at his throat, two Hmong rifles pressed to his face. Noone hisses into his ear.

> NOONE
> (in Vietnamese)
> One sound and you are dead.

NVA SOLDIERS smoke on the trail. Truck engines idle.

NOONE removes his hand as Tranh slaps tape across Han's mouth. Noone jerks Han to his feet and pulls him into the jungle. Han grabs almost comically at his pants.

An NVA SOLDIER peers in from the road.

NVA SOLDIER

Colonel?

NOONE hears him and stops. There is no insignia on Han's uniform.

NOONE

Colonel?

Han's expression is frozen. Noone quickly ties his hands in a way that allows movement, then whips out his knife and slits a small opening in the tape over his mouth. Breath escapes, and a trickle of blood. Noone speaks to him in breathless Vietnamese.

NOONE

You will run when we run.

Noone loops a rope around Han's neck as a leash.

NOONE

And if you fall behind...

Noone takes a 9mm from his pocket and presses the barrel between Han's eyes.

NOONE

Got it?

Han is impassive. Noone CRACKS his cheek with the gun—hard.

NOONE

Got it?!

Han's eyes shoot daggers. He nods. Noone takes the radio from Reeby and straps it on.

NOONE
(into handset)

Rhino, Chimp...

DECKER takes the handset from his radioman.

                    DECKER

     Rhino.

INTERCUT NOONE/DECKER

                    NOONE
     I got one. Get out of there.

                    DECKER
     Say again?

                    NOONE
     They're gonna miss him in about a fucking
     minute. It's a colonel.

                    DECKER
     You're shitting me!

                    NOONE
     We'll talk later.

                    DECKER
     Head straight for extraction. We'll meet you.

An NVA SOLDIER cautiously approaches the spot where Colonel
Han disappeared.

                    NVA SOLDIER
     Colonel?

He sees the dropped toilet paper.

                    NVA SOLDIER
     The Colonel's gone!

An NVA CAPTAIN on the trail throws down his cigarette.

                    NVA CAPTAIN
                (to himself)
     Americans...
                (loud)
     Up, up! Let's go!

NOONE AND HIS STRIKERS push through jungle with both caution and haste, breath audible.

DECKER is on the move. He speaks into his radio.

> DECKER
> Buster Brown, this is Harvard Truant.

> RADIO RELAY (O.S.)
> (from radio)
> Brown, over.

> DECKER
> Get the choppers up. We're headed for extraction.

NOONE checks his compass as he weaves through foliage, radio handset clipped to his shoulder strap, listening in.

> RADIO RELAY (O.S.)
> (from Noone's handset)
> Roger, choppers coming.

> DECKER (O.S.)
> (from Noone's handset)
> And call in air. We've got trucks on the trail.

> RADIO RELAY (O.S.)
> (from Noone's handset)
> Roger, air on the way.

NVA SOLDIERS form up like a posse on the trail, then push into the jungle after their Colonel.

DECKER and his men move through dense foliage…

NOONE hurries the prisoner along…

AN NVA AMBUSH ! waits in expectant silence.

NOONE slashes through foliage…

THE NVA AMBUSH becomes more alert. One of them hears something and signals...

DECKER leads his men along a narrow path...

THE NVA POSSE moves relentlessly ahead...

NOONE pulls Han by the rope...

THE NVA AMBUSH prepares to open fire — but on WHO?!

DECKER moves cautiously through a slightly open area. There's a faint metallic CLICK. His eyes flash a second before the patrol is torn into by MASSIVE GUNFIRE. Decker is hit as he returns fire.

NOONE hears the ambush from a distance.

THE NVA POSSE also hears it.

DECKER and his strikers are ripped apart by loud relentless fire. Bullets tear the shirts of motionless men... Finally, the barrage withers and stops.

NOONE growls into his radio.

                    NOONE
          Rhino! Rhino!

DECKER'S RADIOMAN lies dead, eyes open. The handset crackles.

                    NOONE (O.S.)
               (from radio)
          Rhino...!

THE NVA POSSE moves towards the ambush.

NOONE looks at Colonel Han. He is torn between his duty to deliver the prisoner, and his concern for his friend. He quickly ties Han to a tree and motions to his strikers.

THE NVA AMBUSH SOLDIERS walk among the dead and dying.

DECKER is wounded bad. He weakly tries to raise his rifle.

DECKER'S P.O.V. as an NVA soldier enters frame and casually SHOOTS him. The crack of the rifle is unusual, as if the shot that kills you sounds different.

DECKER'S P.O.V ANGLE shifts as his head drops back. The view of jungle and soldiers remains, but gradually takes on an OTHERWORLDLY AURA. A few gunshots are heard as the NVA make sure everyone is dead. They sound muffled, harmless...

NOONE and his strikers creep up to see the NVA soldiers searching bodies. DECKER'S BODY lies at an odd angle. An unpleasant-looking NVA SERGEANT stoops to search it. He sees the "Cut on dotted line" tattoo on his neck and laughs.

> NVA SERGEANT
> (in Vietnamese)
> Look what it says. Anybody else read English?

THE NVA SOLDIERS gather around Decker's body.

NOONE, jaw clenched, takes in the scene.

> NOONE
> (to himself)
> They're bunching up.

Noone takes grenades from his web gear and motions his strikers do the same.

AN NVA SOLDIER bends to read the tattoo.

> NVA SOLDIER
> (in English)
> "Cut on dotted line."
> (in Vietnamese)
> Cut on dotted line!

Everyone laughs. The NVA Sergeant motions for a MACHETE. He sneers a grin and bows to Decker's body.

NVA SERGEANT
(raising the machete)
As you wish.

DECKER'S AFTER-DEATH P.O.V as the blade comes down. The P.O.V. angle shifts. Then RISES...

THE NVA SERGEANT stands holding Decker's HEAD.

NOONE and his men pull the first pins on their grenades, then throw-pull-throw as fast as they can. Each lobs three grenades, then flattens.

THE NVA SOLDIERS have mixed reactions to Decker's head. Some laugh, others look away. Grenades drop in. One bounces off a soldier and EXPLODES. More explosions send BODIES FLYING.

NOONE and his strikers rush in, rifles blazing. Wounded NVA soldiers crawl away. Bullets tear into them.

THE NVA POSSEE moves cautiously towards the gunfire.

NOONE empties clip after clip, then grabs an AK-47 from the ground and empties it, then another. He's impressive.

The STRIKERS do the same only not as fast or as well.

NOONE'S P.O.V. reveals a time-synch mismatch as the NVA move in slow-motion compared to Noone's efficient speed and flawless anticipation. He's "in the zone."

The STRIKERS empty weapon after weapon until finally they stop, still looking everywhere at once, not quite believing they could have gotten them all.

THE NVA POSSE seems even bigger now as soldiers converge from everywhere and head towards Noone's position.

NOONE stands motionless, transfixed, staring into nothing as if it were the FACE OF GOD...

NOONE'S P.O.V. radiates with transparent clarity as his experience of being in the zone progresses into a visionary, TRANSCENDENT STATE, not unlike Decker's after-death P.O.V.

As he looks around, the vision intensifies—light shifts, colors morph, the air fractures and vibrates... Everything is transformed, and utterly... BEAUTIFUL! His gaze rests on Decker's head looking serenely back at him.

REEBY sees Noone is not himself.

> REEBY
> Sajen Noone! Chimpanzee!

NOONE stares at him, then takes a rucksack from a dead striker and stuffs in Decker's head as he absently gives orders.

> NOONE
> (flat, auto-pilot)
> Guns, clips, smoke...

THE NVA POSSE moves more quickly now.

NOONE and his men take guns and equipment from the dead.

BAAP CANH listens to the jungle.

> BAAP CANH
> Coming!

The air suddenly cracks with bullets. TRANH takes one in the forehead and drops like a stone.

> NOONE
> Tranh!

NOONE is shocked to normal awareness.

> NOONE
> Go! Go!

He snatches up the rucksack with Decker's head as they take off.

NOONE stops to cut Colonel Han from the tree. Their eyes lock and hold. Something is different now...

> BAAP CANH
> Coming!

NOONE shakes it off and pushes Han ahead of him.

THE NVA POSSE arrives at the ambush site. The Captain eyes the carnage.

> NVA CAPTAIN
> Get them!

NOONE'S GROUP runs hard. They come to a steep slope and slide down, bouncing off trees and roots, then keep running.

> NOONE
> (into radio)
> Buster Brown, Harvard Truant. You got choppers up?

> RADIO RELAY (O.S.)
> (from radio)
> Roger, and your airstrike's coming.

> NOONE
> (into radio)
> Where's those choppers?!

IN A CLEAR SKY two HUEYS beat the air.

> HUEY PILOT
> Right here, Truant. This is Dragonfly, headed for extraction.

INTERCUT NOONE/HUEY PILOT

> NOONE
> Can't make it. Running. Hot as shit.

> HUEY PILOT
> Where are you?

NOONE pops and drops a smoke grenade without breaking stride.

> NOONE
> Popping smoke.

THE HUEY PILOT sees nothing but a vast expanse of dense green jungle. Then in the far distance, yellow smoke.

> HUEY PILOT
> I have yellow smoke.

> NOONE
> Roger yellow. Which way to an LZ?

> HUEY PILOT
> Nothing in site. Have to be McGuire.

> NOONE
> (checking compass)
> Heading one-one-zero. Only four of us left.

> HUEY PILOT
> Roger. One of us will snag you, the other cover.

THE NVA POSSE arrives at the steep slope and maneuvers down.

NOONE stops his group to quickly run a long trip wire attached to a smoke grenade, then they take off running again, breathing hard.

THE NVA POSSE is in hot pursuit.

NOONE looks up as he runs, scanning the thick canopy for an opening. Choppers thwock in the distance.

> NOONE
> I hear you.

> HUEY PILOT
> Pop smoke when you find a hole.

                              NOONE
          Thick as shit.

                           HUEY PILOT
          We don't need much. Let's get you out of there.

THE NVA CAPTAIN hears the choppers.

                          NVA CAPTAIN
          Let's go, let's go! Hurry!

NOONE'S GROUP runs as fast as the jungle will allow, looking up,
desperate to find an opening.

IN A CLEAR SKY drone two single-prop A1-E SKYRAIDERS,
looking as if they belong in WWII.

INTERCUT NOONE/HUEY PILOT/A1-E PILOT

                           A1-E PILOT
          Harvard Truant, this is Cakewalk. Somebody
          say something about trucks on the trail?

NOONE scans the thick canopy for an opening.

                              NOONE
          Change in plans. Stand by.

                           HUEY PILOT
          Talk to me, Truant.

Colonel Han stumbles. Noone jerks him to his feet.

                              NOONE
            Working it.

THE NVA POSSE is close. One of them hits the trip wire and RED
SMOKE rises.

NOONE finds a small opening in the canopy.

NOONE
All right, Dragonfly. Here we go...

HUEY PILOT
Where are you? Give me some smoke.

NOONE AND HIS STRIKERS frantically search their gear for a smoke grenade. They can't find one!

HUEY PILOT
Okay, roger. I see red smoke.

NOONE
No! Not red! Not red! Cakewalk, fire on red!

AI-E PILOT
Roger. Fire on red.

NOONE finally finds a smoke grenade—in the rucksack with Decker's head! He pops it and throws it high above the canopy.

HUEY PILOT
I have blue smoke.

NOONE
Blue, blue! Come on! Come on!

THE SKYRAIDERS fly low over red smoke. BOMBS drop. THE NVA POSSE is showered with white phosphorous as bombs EXPLODE in treetops. Some are hit and fall screaming to the ground, hot particles burning.

NVA CAPTAIN
Get out of the smoke! Go! Go!

NOONE and his men face back the way they came, rifles aimed. The sound of a HUEY gets louder as it appears overhead.

NOONE
You're here! Drop 'em!

The upper canopy swirls. Four harnesses tumble down. Noone hooks up Colonel Han as the strikers strap in.

                         NOONE
          Cakewalk, split red and blue!

                        A1-E PILOT
          Roger. Splitting red and blue.

THE SKYRAIDERS come around again and drop bombs between the red and blue smoke. Again the NVA are hit hard. Explosions send bodies flying.

                       NVA CAPTAIN
               Get up! Go! Go!

NOONE straps himself into the last harness.

                         NOONE
          We're in, Dragonfly! Let's go!

THE HUEY ascends, pulling the four men up through the trees.

THE NVA POSSE runs towards Noone's position.

NOONE'S GROUP nears the top of the opening, branches lashing and tugging at them. Finally they clear the trees.

                         NOONE
               Clear! Go! Go!

THE NVA POSSE runs into the BLUE SMOKE just as the dangling men disappear above the canopy. They fire in their direction.

THE HUEY banks and gains altitude, four MEN DANGLING.

NOONE'S P.O.V. as he looks down over his boots at the receding smoke, GREEN TRACERS streaking past.

                         NOONE
          Cakewalk, fire on blue!

A1-E PILOT
        Roger, fire on blue.

THE SKYRAIDERS take a run over blue smoke. Napalm canisters tumble to earth. The jungle erupts into a massive orange INFERNO.

INSIDE THE INFERNO bodies burst into flame.

THE OTHER HUEY fires rockets and machine gun tracers into the firestorm.

NOONE'S P.O.V. as the burning jungle recedes...

THE HUEY fades into the distance. The DANGLING MEN disappear into a clear and silent sky...

<u>ACT II</u>: NOONE'S ROOM IN THE MIKE FORCE TEAMHOUSE

Jimi Hendrix, "Wind Cries Mary" fades up. Candles light a room littered with combat gear, muddy boots, weapons, glamour magazines, women's shoes...

In an open armoire the clothes of an American soldier hang alongside the robes and dresses of a Vietnamese woman.

On a painted oriental dresser, cosmetics mingle with hand grenades and ammo clips. Incense sticks smolder before a statue of BUDDHA. Next to Buddha, in the dresser mirror, is the REFLECTION of a naked woman in rhythmic motion.

The woman is KIM, 20, an attractive Vietnamese. She moves erotically astride a naked man face down on the bed. It's NOONE.

Slowly and sensuously Kim slides herself over him, her hands kneading his back and shoulders. Close-ups. Extreme close-ups. She massages him with her whole body. Noone rolls over beneath her. They are nose to nose and her motion stops. Then begins again...

THE NEXT MORNING Kim stirs awake. Through an open window, the sound of a bird. Beside her Noone sleeps. She gets out of bed and stands naked, absently watching a lizard on the window sill. She slips into a robe and lights an incense stick for Buddha.

IN THE MIKE FORCE TEAMHOUSE BATHROOM

Staff Sergeant DAN STILES, black, twenties, shaves in his underwear at one of several sinks.

Sergeant PAUL RENFROW, twenties, towel at his waist, shaves at another. Sound of showers.

                         RENFROW
          Yeah, but with a tattoo like that...

                          STILES
          You can't blame the tattoo.

KIM strolls past them to a row of toilet stalls with dividers but no doors. In the first sits MAI, a young Vietnamese woman, reading a magazine. [*They converse in Vietnamese.*]

                           KIM
          Morning.

                           MAI
          Morning.

In the next stall a soldier in olive-drab boxers stands urinating. The third stall is empty. Kim sits.

THREE-SHOT OF STALLS

                      RENFROW (O.S.)
          But it's like asking for it.

                           MAI
          Kim?

                           KIM
          Hmm?

                           MAI
          You going to town today?

                    STILES (O.S.)
          He was already dead so it's a moot point.

                         KIM
            Yes, I have shopping.

The soldier in the middle stall flushes and leaves.

                         MAI
          I'll go with you, okay?

                    RENFROW (O.S.)
          Don't fuck with the cosmos, is all I'm saying.

                         KIM
                    (in English)
          Okay, no sweat.

KIM flushes and goes to the sink to wash up. Renfrow grins at her.

                       RENFROW
          When you get tired of Noone, I'm all yours, baby.

Kim dries her hands on the towel at his waist, then pulls it off and
lets it drop, giving his package a casual glance.

                         KIM
          Never happen.

Stiles busts a gut. Renfrow picks up his towel.

THE MIKE FORCE TEAMHOUSE COMMON ROOM

Comfortably furnished living and dining areas, pool table, bar,
jukebox, ceiling fans—the feel of a rustic clubhouse. A TV airs the
"Today Show."

A dozen Special Forces (SF) soldiers and several Vietnamese women
eat breakfast at small tables with white tablecloths.

NOONE enters from a side hallway in faded jungle fatigues. He
steps behind the bar and makes a Bloody Maria.

Stiles and Renfrow, dressed for operation in tiger fatigues, sit at a table with Kim, her short robe leaving little to the imagination. Renfrow reads "Stars and Stripes."

> RENFROW
> Look at this. Whole shitload of people showed
> up outside the Pentagon protesting the war.
> Government called out the Guard on 'em.
> (pokes a news photo)
> Girls sticking flowers down rifle barrels. Look at
> the tits on that one…

NOONE sits down with his drink, mind elsewhere.

> STILES
> You all right?

> NOONE
> Yeah.

> STILES
> Your coordinates are good. We'll find 'em.

> NOONE
> I know.

> STILES
> And if not, at least we've got something to bury.

> NOONE
> (slight smile)
> Fuck you.

> STILES
> Seriously. You were sterile — no tags. It was
> good thinking.

> NOONE
> Thinking had nothing to do with it.

THE TV now shows footage of Hmong villagers in Vietnam. An SF SOLDIER turns up the VOLUME. Everyone is suddenly interested.

RENFROW
Hey, they're doing a thing on the 'Yards.

STILES
About fucking time. Nobody in the States knows
they exist.

TV GUEST (V.O.)
(from TV)
These people occupy the Central Highlands,
which are highly strategic to both sides in the
war.

ON TV the film clip ends. A male GUEST is being interviewed by the
HOST of the "Today Show."

TV HOST
So how long did you live with them?

TV GUEST
About a year — with Rhade and Jarai tribes.

TV HOST
(to O.S. crew)
Can we go to the next clip?

THE NEXT CLIP shows more scenes of Hmong village life.

TV HOST (V.O.)
They are the original people of Vietnam?

TV GUEST (V.O.)
Yes. They call themselves Hmong, or Degar. The
French called them Montagnards, "mountain
people," which has continued with the
Americans.

ON THE FILM a scene shows South Vietnamese Army (ARVN)
soldiers bullying Hmong villagers.

                    TV GUEST (V.O.)
The Vietnamese word for the Hmong means
"savages" and that's pretty much how they are
treated by the South Vietnamese government.
Hanoi is no better.

THE FILM cuts to a distinguished Hmong man in military fatigues
being treated with deference and affection by Hmong villagers.

                    TV HOST (V.O.)
And this is...?

                    TV GUEST (V.O.)
General Y-Bham Enoul, commander of FULRO,
the Hmong revolutionary army. He led the
failed uprising in 1964 and now operates out of
Cambodia.

                    TV HOST (V.O.)
What do they want?

                    TV GUEST (V.O.)
Restoration of an independent homeland.

                    TV HOST (V.O.)
Restoration?

                    TV GUEST (V.O.)
Yes. Under the French, the Hmong had their
own sovereign territory.

THE FILM cuts to a series of shots of SF SOLDIERS training Hmong
troops, dispensing medical treatment, eating with villagers...

                    TV HOST (V.O.)
We know the U.S. Special Forces works closely
with these people...

A CHEER goes up in the teamhouse.

                    TV GUEST (V.O.)
Yes, but every Montagnard's first loyalty is to
FULRO—

                    TV HOST (V.O.)
Which is considered an enemy by the South
Vietnamese government.

The film clip ends.

                    TV GUEST
Yes. It's a delicate and potentially explosive
situation.

                    TV HOST
Yet insiders say Montagnard support is the key
to the war.

                    TV GUEST
Absolutely. They occupy the most strategic area
of Southeast Asia—the Central Highlands.
Whoever wins the Highlands, wins Vietnam.

The TV segment ends as Captain STEVE MONROE, black, late
thirties, dressed for operation, walks into the team room. Physically
he is not impressive. He has had to prove himself his whole life.

                    MONROE
Rich boy, Colonel called. Wants to see you.

                    STILES
Uh-oh. Principal's office.

                    MONROE
Stiles, Renfrow, let's go.

They leave. Kim studies the photo of women putting flowers in rifles
at the Pentagon. She cups her breasts as if weighing them.

                    KIM
I go shopping today.

Noone takes a pull at his drink.

                         NOONE
          I need new sandals.

                         KIM
          Okay, no sweat.

IN THE MIKE FORCE COMPOUND

NOONE emerges from the teamhouse. A small crew of Hmong strikers digs footings for an addition. Supervising is Sergeant First Class Diego "BIG MARTY" Martinez, late thirties, an imposing, immediately likable man with a wide smile.

                         MARTY
                    (to strikers)
          A little deeper over here.

Noone gestures at the size of the foundation.

                         NOONE
          Jesus, Marty. Expecting company?

                         MARTY
          Scrounged a huge mahogany bar. Had to build
          to fit.

                         NOONE
          Be one hell of a club.

                         MARTY
          Any luck we'll have it finished for Tet. Christen
          it big.

Noone climbs into a jeep and cranks it.

ON A RURAL ROAD IN VIETNAM

NOONE drives slowly past huts and small houses. Each passing FACE holds a story...

He approaches the gate of a large U.S. compound. Hmong guards let him through. He parks in front of a building topped with a large sign: "Headquarters, 5th Special Forces Group (Airborne), Vietnam."

IN THE COMMANDER'S OFFICE

Colonel JOHN PULLMAN, 5th SFG commanding officer, reads reports at his desk. Buzzed head, powerful build — a man you don't want to fuck with. He motions to a chair as NOONE enters.

> PULLMAN
> How's things at Mike Force?

> NOONE
> Good, sir.

> PULLMAN
> Getting what you need?

> NOONE
> Yes, sir, thanks to Marty. He's even building a
> new club.

> PULLMAN
> (grudging admiration)
> Balls of a cat-burglar. I had a case of single-malt
> disappear a couple months back. Knew it was
> Marty, but couldn't prove it.

> NOONE
> What label?

> PULLMAN
> Macallan 18.

> NOONE
> Nice.

> PULLMAN
> You know scotch?

                              NOONE
Maybe too well.

                             PULLMAN
What's your preference?

                              NOONE
Most any good highland, but if I had to drink
the same thing every night, Oban.

                             PULLMAN
Kinda young to be a whiskey expert.

                              NOONE
My father collects single malts like others collect
wine. I started helping myself at an early age.

Pullman opens a desk drawer and pours two drinks without letting
Noone see the bottle. He hands one to Noone.

                             PULLMAN
Impress me.

Noone checks color, sniffs, sips a couple times.

                              NOONE
Lagavulin 16. I'm not a big fan of Islays, usually.
Too medicinal. But this is the best of them.

                             PULLMAN
Motherfucker.

Pullman produces his bottle of Lagavulin 16 and pours them each
another finger.

                             PULLMAN
Goddamn shame about Decker.

                              NOONE
Yes, sir.

                    PULLMAN
Not much detail in your report.

                    NOONE
I'm glad to answer questions.

                    PULLMAN
I'm not second-guessing. Just a goddamn
shame, that's all.

                    NOONE
Yes, sir.

                    PULLMAN
Hell of a snatch, though, Noone. A goddamn
colonel.

                    NOONE
He found *me*.

                    PULLMAN
It's what you do with opportunity that counts.

                    NOONE
Things just started happening.

                    PULLMAN
You need to learn how to take a compliment, son.

                    NOONE
Yes, sir.

Pullman re-lights a half-smoked cigar.

                    PULLMAN
Decker was due to start working for the Agency
directly.

                    NOONE
Yes, sir. Something with FULRO.

                    PULLMAN
    He told you?

                    NOONE
    That's all he said.

                    PULLMAN
    This needs to be kept quiet and unnoticed,
    Noone. Understood?

                    NOONE
    Yes, sir.

                    PULLMAN
    Cobb recommended you take Decker's place.
    You'll still bunk over at Mike Force, just have a
    different job. You okay with that?

Noone's expression is complex. Before his transcendent experience in
the jungle, this would have been a dream assignment. Now things
aren't so clear. He hesitates.

                    PULLMAN
    Is there a problem?

                    NOONE
    No, sir. I'm okay with that.

                    PULLMAN
    Good. Get up with Cobb. He'll take it from here.
    You'll be working for Carter Jakes. Consider his
    orders my orders.

                    NOONE
    Yes, sir.

Noone downs his drink and stands. Pullman returns to his papers.
Noone pauses at the door.

                    PULLMAN
    Something else?

                              NOONE
Where are they holding the NVA colonel?

                              PULLMAN
MAC-V compound.

                              NOONE
I was wondering if I might see him.

                              PULLMAN
Why?

                              NOONE
I'm not sure.

Pullman considers.

                              PULLMAN
I'll make a call.

IN A MACV PRISON CELL

COLONEL HAN sits motionless on his bunk staring at the floor. At
the sound of the door he looks up. NOONE is let in. They stare at
each other.

                              COLONEL HAN
                          (excellent English)
                 You've joined the interrogations?

                              NOONE
No. I just came to talk.

                              COLONEL HAN
About what?

                              NOONE
I don't know. Talk.

                              COLONEL HAN
Relive old times?

                    NOONE
No, I just—

                    COLONEL HAN
Perhaps you think our shared experience has
formed a bond.

                    NOONE
I have no—

                    COLONEL HAN
We did not share anything, Sergeant. To you I'm
a trophy in your adventure—

                    NOONE
That's not—

                    COLONEL HAN
To me, you are the cause and witness of my
humiliation.

With a resigned nod, Noone takes several packs of cigarettes from his
pockets and tosses them on Han's bunk.

                    NOONE
I feel stupid. You probably don't even smoke.

He knocks on the door to be let out. Han opens a pack of cigarettes,
takes one, offers the pack to Noone. An MP opens the door.

                    NOONE
Never mind.

The MP shuts the door. Noone takes a cigarette. He flicks open his
lighter and lights their smokes. Noone's lighter bears the INSIGNIA
of an NVA military unit. Han notes it.

                    COLONEL HAN
I served in that unit for awhile.

                    NOONE
Keep it.

Han looks Noone over, then slips the lighter into his pocket. Noone gestures to the bruise on Han's cheek.

> NOONE
> I'm sorry I hit you.

> COLONEL HAN
> Me too.

> NOONE
> Are they treating you well?

> COLONEL HAN
> As well as can be expected.

> NOONE
> Your English is remarkable.

> COLONEL HAN
> Berkeley, class of '52.

> NOONE
> No shit?

> COLONEL HAN
> I lived in America for twelve years.

> NOONE
> But here you are.

> COLONEL HAN
> I don't agree with my government on many things. Philosophically, I'm probably not even communist. But in the end, this is my home. All of it.

> NOONE
> Robert E. Lee...

> COLONEL HAN
> What?

> NOONE
An American Civil War general.

> COLONEL HAN
I know who he is.

> NOONE
He had a similar decision.

> COLONEL HAN
Thank you for the comparison.

They smoke in silence.

> NOONE
I'm sorry it was you.

> COLONEL HAN
When you cut me from the tree... It seemed for a moment you might let me go.

> NOONE
Yes. Something happened.

> COLONEL HAN
I heard.

> NOONE
I mean... to me.

> COLONEL HAN
Your eyes were different. What was it?

> NOONE
(drifts inward)
I don't know... The world... shifted.

> COLONEL HAN
Shifted?

                    NOONE
              (pokes his chest)
     Like everything was right here. Like God and
     the whole fucking universe was right here...

                    COLONEL HAN
     And mine were the first eyes you looked into.

                    NOONE
     Yes...

                    COLONEL HAN
     You religious?

                    NOONE
     No.

                    COLONEL HAN
     You should talk to someone.

                    NOONE
              (ironic smile)
     I guess I am.

                    COLONEL HAN
     Someone religious.

IN THE MIKE FORCE TEAMHOUSE

A dozen SF SOLDIERS listen reverently, along with KIM, MAI, and a
few other Vietnamese women. FRANK COBB stands behind the bar,
on which rests Decker's GREEN BERET and a MEMORIAL PLAQUE
that matches twenty others on the wall behind.

                    COBB
              (continuing)
     Lyle Decker had three full tours in Nam, and
     fuck knows how many extensions — not even
     counting coming on TDY from Okinawa.

NOONE listens.

COBB

He never cared about rank — up and down like a
yo-yo. Used to say, "If I had all my promotions
and none of my busts I'd be on my third term as
President."

People smile.

COBB

Stepped in a lot of shit together, me and Decker.
Flat out saved my life once in Laos. He was a
good friend and a good soldier. Loved what he
did and died doing it. Can't ask for more than
that in life… That's about it for what I've got to
say.

Cobb reads from a well-worn Bible.

COBB

"The Lord is my shepherd, I shall not want.
He maketh me to lie down in green pastures.
He leadeth me beside the still waters.
He restoreth my soul. He leadeth me in the path
of righteousness for his name's sake.
Yea, though I walk through the valley of the
shadow of death, I shall fear no evil,
for thou art with me. Thy rod and thy staff,
they comfort me."

Noone is deeply moved, surprising him.

COBB

"Thou preparest a table before me
in the presence of my enemies.
Thou anointest my head with oil.
My cup runneth over.
Surely goodness and mercy shall follow me
all the days of my life, and I will dwell
in the house of the Lord, forever."

IN NOONE'S ROOM

NOONE sits motionless on the edge of the bed, his profile incidentally reflected in the mirror next to Buddha. There's a gentle KNOCK. Noone seems not to hear. A young Hmong MAID glides in with an armload of folded laundry.

                    MAID
        Sorry.

She leaves the laundry and closes the door behind her. Noone continues to stare into nothing.

ON A BEACH IN VIETNAM AT NIGHT

A full moon shimmers on dark water. Waves break on pale sand beneath gently swaying palms...

In the foreground, a JEEP flashes by.

The jeep is driven by COBB, NOONE shotgun. Civilian clothes. They pass Noone's FLASK, warm wind in their faces.

                    NOONE
        Good eulogy.

                    COBB
        I'm not much for speaking.

                    NOONE
        You read that psalm like a preacher.

                    COBB
        You must never been around preachers.

                    NOONE
        You religious?

                    COBB
        I wouldn't say I wasn't.

                              NOONE
               Know much about it?

                              COBB
               Fuck no. Nobody does.

                              NOONE
               Do you think it's possible to know?

                              COBB
               What is it with you tonight?

                              NOONE
                    (beat)
               Nothing.

ON A MOONLIT BEACH ROAD the jeep disappears into darkness.

IN A CITY IN VIETNAM AT NIGHT

COBB and NOONE open the door of a large building. Next to it, a
brass sign is engraved "Club Paris." From inside, live JAZZ.

INSIDE CLUB PARIS two Chinese BOUNCERS in white dinner
jackets nod them through.

                              COBB
               Ever been in here?

                              NOONE
               No.

                              COBB
                    (grins)
               Well, you're in it now.

Cobb leads Noone through double doors into the main salon. The
complex ambiance is a heady blend of Paris brothel, Shanghai bar,
Harlem night club, Rick's Cafe Americain... The patrons are well
dressed Asians and western men with the look of the underworld.
Attractive prostitutes mingle. The place exudes danger, intrigue,
romance. The year could as easily be 1937 as 1967.

At a large table, subtly presiding, is MADAME YEN, beautiful-but-deadly dragon lady extraordinaire.

Seated next to her is SUONG LE, now 18, demure, sensual, even more beautiful. Her long raven hair falls across her back. Around her neck, a black velvet choker with cameo.

Ever watchful of her domain, Madame Yen regards Noone as he enters. Her gaze lingers approvingly. She sees that Suong Le has also taken notice of him. Of this she does not approve.

CARTER JAKES sits at a corner table with two hard-edged Vietnamese men.

                    JAKES
          Which is why we can't stand around on our
          fucking dicks in the meantime, goddamn it!

He glances up as Cobb and Noone approach. With a gesture from Jakes, the others stand, give curt nods, and move off.

                    COBB
          Carter Jakes, Randy Noone.

Noone extends his hand. Jakes regards him as he takes it.

                    JAKES
          Like the ancients used to say, "If your champion
          dies in battle, hire the one who carries his head."

                    NOONE
                (bristling slightly)
          Which ancients were those?

                    JAKES
          Fuck if I know. I might have made it up.

A WAITRESS takes drink orders, leaves. In the silence that follows, Noone speaks first. Jakes smiles. To him, everything is meaningful.

                    NOONE
          Interesting crowd.

                              JAKES
              Tell me something about them.

                              NOONE
              Like what?

                              JAKES
              Anything.

Noone takes a casual look around.

                              NOONE
              I don't know. Money, power...

His eyes come to rest on Madame Yen and Suong Le.

                              NOONE
              Beautiful women…

                              JAKES
              Politicians, bankers, mandarins, gangsters—
              even a few communists. Most of them know
              each other, and outside this room they may even
              be enemies.

Noone shrugs, uncertain what is being asked. Jakes gestures he should look again.

                              JAKES
              They share a common interest.

Noone studies the room. Each FACE holds a story...

                              NOONE
              Opium.

                              JAKES
                      (grinning at Cobb)
              See what a 160 IQ does for you?

CHAU, an attractive young prostitute with a beauty mark reminiscent of Marilyn Monroe, glides up.

                              CHAU
            Hello, Frank. How you be?

The waitress brings drinks. Cobb downs his.

                              COBB
            If you gentlemen will excuse us. I know you
            need to get acquainted.

He tosses the jeep key to Noone.

                              COBB
            Pick me up here in the morning.

He and Chau move off.

                              JAKES
            Interesting file, yours. One year Harvard, three
            years Nam. Unusual ratio for a son of privilege.

                              NOONE
            Is that a question?

                              JAKES
            Your daddy's rich and your mama's good
            looking.

                              NOONE
                        (dueling quotes)
            God bless the child that's got his own.

                              JAKES
            You turn down football scholarships to go to
            Harvard, then suddenly quit Harvard to go SF
            and spook around the jungle.

                              NOONE
            Things change.

                              JAKES
            By now you'd be graduated, married to trophy
            pussy, and next in line to run the family empire.

                    NOONE
You asking why?

                    JAKES
I'm asking why.

                    NOONE
              (offhand but sincere)
Just seemed there must be more to it, that's all.

                    JAKES
More to what?

                    NOONE
I don't know. Life.

                    JAKES
Kinda vague.

                    NOONE
Okay, my father. I didn't want to live my
father's life. That Freudian enough for you?

                    JAKES
I heard you weren't much for details.

                    NOONE
Controlling, ruthless, manipulative...

                    JAKES
All of which was apparently fine with you until
the end of freshman year.

                    NOONE
              (shrugs)
What can I tell ya.

                    JAKES
You walked away from the life of a prince into a
line of work with a really shitty survival rate.
How about you tell me who the fuck I'm about
to hire.

                    NOONE
I'm not crazy, if that's what you want to know. I
just like who I am when I'm here.

                    JAKES
Who are you?

                    NOONE
I guess that's everyone's big question, isn't it?

Jakes sips his drink.

                    JAKES
It must have been hard, your girlfriend dying
like that. Seems like your father could have
afforded a better abortion doctor.

Noone looks like he's been kicked in the stomach.

                    NOONE
How the fuck...?

                    JAKES
                (stating the obvious)
        CIA...?

Noone is all out of bravado. He slumps in his chair.

                    NOONE
My father had my life all mapped out for me.
Congressman, senator... Had me believing it was
what I wanted, too. He'd run for Congress a
couple times but even with all his money he lost.
Blamed it on not having an education. Eighth
grade dropout. Saw me as his redemption.

                    JAKES
So you gave up football to get Harvard on your
resume.

                    NOONE
Yeah.

                              JAKES

And the girl?

                             NOONE

High school sweethearts. Classic quarterback
and cheerleader cliché. We were in serious love.
Gonna get married after I finished college…

Noone stares at his hands in silence for a long moment.

                             NOONE

My father thought she was low class — not a
good politician's wife. Didn't want his plans for
me disrupted… Her father was a blue-collar
alcoholic. My father used that to get his way.
Gave him a shitload of money to make his
daughter get an abortion… And the greedy son-
of-bitch still got the cheapest fucking quack he
could find!

                              JAKES

Not your fault.

                             NOONE

Yes it was. I should have known something was
wrong. I should have got her out of that house. I
left her alone to deal with her goddamn
drunken father…

Noone takes a long pull at his drink.

                              JAKES

What about your mother?

                             NOONE

She wanted grandkids so bad she didn't care
about anything else. Supported me in wanting
to get married right then. Even gave me my
grandmother's engagement ring to… I never got
the… fucking father…

                    JAKES
So now you're going to spite him by getting
yourself killed.

                    NOONE
I work hard to stay alive.

                    JAKES
You just plan to keep doing hairy ops until the
day that's not enough.

                    NOONE
I'm still here.

Jakes nods almost imperceptibly.

                    JAKES
                (moving forward)
Cobb says you speak better 'Yard than he does.
That takes some doing.

                    NOONE
Languages come easy.

                    JAKES
Know what FULRO stands for?

                    NOONE
Front Unifie de Lutte des Races Opprimees. "United
Front for the Liberation of Oppressed Races."

                    JAKES
Seem like a good cause to you?

                    NOONE
I'm all for liberation.

The WAITRESS arrives with another round. Jakes appraises Noone
as she serves. When she leaves, he gets down to it.

                         JAKES
Infiltration from the North is out of control. If it
isn't stopped soon there'll be no way to win this
fucker. Public opinion in the States is turning
hard against us.

                         NOONE
What's FULRO got to do with it?

                         JAKES
A sovereign Hmong nation separating North
and South Vietnam may be the only way we get
out of this war without our tail between our
legs. It's not just Vietnam. We've got indigenous
forces in Cambodia, Laos... Shit, we've got secret
armies coming out the ass. We just need to get
them all fighting for the same thing.

                         NOONE
What about Saigon?

                         JAKES
Without a Montagnard state as buffer, the South
will eventually fall.

                         NOONE
So, I'd be what, training FULRO troops?

                         JAKES
That's being covered. You'd work with me and
Cobb at a higher level. Negotiations, financing...
Bodyguard with brains.

                         NOONE
Financing?

Jakes leans back and gestures vaguely.

                         JAKES
That table you keep looking at? The older
woman is Ngo Linh Yen — Madame Yen. Second
biggest opium player in Vietnam.

SUONG LE glances up to see NOONE looking. Their eyes catch and hold. She looks shyly away.

                    NOONE
          And the biggest?

Jakes nods towards another table. Seated there is GENERAL TONG in a white linen suit, flanked by several goons.

                    JAKES
          General Nguyen Van Tong, South Vietnamese
          Air Force. Number one with a bullet.

TONG sees them looking and flashes a reptilian grin. Jakes smiles insincerely and tips his glass.

                    JAKES
               (*soto voce*)
          Eat shit and die, motherfucker.

                    NOONE
          You're in the opium business.

                    JAKES
          Hard not to be. It's run by the Saigon elite we're
          here to support, and grown by the tribes we
          need as allies.

Noone lights a smoke. His thoughts turn inward. The lights dim as MUSIC fades up—the intro to a familiar song...

                    NOONE
          So in the middle of a war you're going to stage a
          revolution and re-draw the borders of three
          countries.

                    JAKES
          When you say it like that, it makes it sound
          hard.

                    BAND LEADER (O.S.)
                      (from mic)
             Mesdames et Messieurs... Pearl.

ON STAGE a microphone stands under a small spotlight. At the
perfect moment, SUONG LE glides up to it and sings "La Vie En
Rose" in French. She has a beautiful voice uniquely her own, yet
somehow she evokes Edith Piaf and days gone by.

At Madame Yen's table she seemed shy, demure. On stage she's a
sultry, mysterious chanteuse, worldly beyond her years. Everyone
stops what they're doing to watch and listen.

She looks at Noone several times as she sings. The total effect of her
beauty, her voice, the music, is mesmerizing. Noone can't take his
eyes off her. His expression is not unlike that during his transcendent
experience in the jungle...

When the song ends she bows to enthusiastic applause, and with a
brief glance at Noone, steps off stage towards the bar. The
BARTENDER pours her a glass of water. NOONE stands.

                        JAKES
            Forget it. She's off limits in more ways than you
            can count.

                        NOONE
            I just want to see what kinds of scotch they have.

AT THE BAR Suong Le senses Noone's arrival but does not look. An
attractive prostitute on the stool between them flashes a smile and
touches Noone's arm. The BARTENDER approaches.

                        NOONE
            Scotch. Something old and expensive.

The bartender seems pleased.

                        BARTENDER
            Very smoky, okay?

                    NOONE
      You're the boss.

Noone looks at Suong Le.

                    NOONE
                (in Vietnamese)
      You have a beautiful voice.

Suong Le does not look at him.

                  SUONG LE
                (in English)
      I have always loved music.

MADAME YEN watches them like a hawk from across the room.
Suong Le feels her eyes.

                    NOONE
      What's your name?

                  SUONG LE
      I am called Pearl.

                    NOONE
      Your real name.

                  SUONG LE
                (hesitates)
      Suong Le.

                    NOONE
      I want to see you.

                  SUONG LE
      That would not be a good idea.

                    NOONE
      You looked at me as if perhaps —

                  SUONG LE
      I look at many people.

58

                              NOONE

Like that?

                              SUONG LE

I must get back.

                              NOONE

I want to see you tomorrow.

                              SUONG LE

I have school—

She glances up at him, suddenly wanting to clarify her age.

                              SUONG LE

College…

Their eyes lock. Neither speaks. Suong Le looks away.

                              SUONG LE

I need to—

                              NOONE

Do you study music? Where's your school?

                              SUONG LE

I must get back.

She moves away. The bartender arrives with Noone's drink. Noone downs it and looks to Madame Yen's table. Madame Yen fusses with Suong Le's hair and speaks to her. Suong Le bows slightly and leaves.

Noone drops money on the bar.

                              NOONE

That's for you. Put the drink on Jakes' tab.

Madame Yen is alone as Noone approaches.

                              NOONE
                         (in Vietnamese)
              She sings beautifully. Will she be back?

                            MADAME YEN
                          (in English)
              Not tonight, no.

She smiles and gestures he join her.

                            MADAME YEN
              Sergeant Noone, isn't it?

                              NOONE
              How would you know that?

                            MADAME YEN
              I know many things.

                              NOONE
              I don't doubt it.

                            MADAME YEN
              She's mine, you know.

                              NOONE
              Your daughter?

                            MADAME YEN
                          (enigmatic smile)
              My ward.

She lowers her eyes then raises them, a changed woman. Her look —
seductive, hypnotic — commands attention.

                            MADAME YEN
              Forget her. Vietnam is full of beautiful women.

Almost in spite of himself, Noone returns her look.

                    NOONE
                (scotch talking)
            Yes, very beautiful.

JAKES appears.

                    JAKES
            Sorry to interrupt.

                    MADAME YEN
            Carter.

                    JAKES
                (to Noone)
            There's a thing we need to do.

Jakes jerks his head towards the door and starts walking ahead.
Noone gets up to follow. Madame Yen touches his hand.

                    MADAME YEN
            Perhaps you could come for lunch tomorrow.
            One-thirty?

ACT III: ON THE STREET OUTSIDE CLUB PARIS

JAKES and NOONE emerge from the club.

                    JAKES
            That fat IQ doesn't kick in when your dick's
            involved, does it?

                    NOONE
            Whose does?

                    JAKES
            Listen, smartass, you're poking at a fucking
            hornets' nest. Madame Yen is a major asset and
            Suong Le belongs to her. Understood? Rule
            number one: Don't shit where you eat.

                    NOONE
            Okay, I get it.

                    JAKES
Make sure you do.

                    NOONE
Look, this isn't going all that well —

                    JAKES
I'll be the judge of that —

                    NOONE
And some weird shit's come up for me lately —

                    JAKES
Welcome to life.

                    NOONE
I'm not right for this job.

                    JAKES
That's the most impressive thing you've said all
night.

Jakes pats his pockets as if looking for glasses. He produces a slightly
bent JOINT and raises an eyebrow in question.

ON A BEACH IN VIETNAM AT NIGHT

JAKES and NOONE recline on the sand, passing the half-smoked
joint. Gentle surf, warm breeze, full moon.

                    NOONE
        Not bad.

                    JAKES
You a connoisseur?

                    NOONE
I know what works.

                    JAKES
There's a little village in Laos I like to drop in on
once in awhile. We'll go sometime.

Noone tokes and passes.

                    NOONE
          I take it Madame Yen's your buyer.

                    JAKES
          Partner, more like.

                    NOONE
          And Tong?

                    JAKES
          He'd like to change that.

                    NOONE
          Do business with both.

                    JAKES
          They're all-or-nothing kind of people. Civil on
          the surface, but underneath… If one of them
          stumbles the other controls the whole market…

Jakes takes a hit.

                    JAKES
          And we can't afford to be on the wrong side if
          that happens.

                    NOONE
          You don't care much for Tong.

                    JAKES
          When you've been here long as I have, you've
          got history with everybody.

                    NOONE
          The coup?

Jakes stares ahead without speaking.

                    NOONE
          Sorry. None of my business.
                  (by way of explanation)
          Seems all the instructors at Intel School have a
          Carter Jakes story. You're a legend in your own
          time.

Jakes allows himself an ironic smile, then reflects.

                    JAKES
          You should have seen this place in the Fifties.
          Still the "Pearl of the Orient." I really thought
          we had a shot at hanging on to that...

FLASHBACK B/W

**JAKES and PRESIDENT DIEM play chess in Diem's lavishly
furnished palace.**

                    JAKES (V.O.)
          **Diem was a pompous mandarin, but
          somewhere along the way we became friends
          of a sort.**

**ON THE STREETS OF SAIGON a protest is underway. Buddhist
monks are in evidence. ARVN soldiers glare at the protesters.**

                    JAKES (V.O.)
          **He listened to his crazy brother too much,
          though. Gave the Catholics all the privileges
          and fucked over the Buddhists.**

BACK TO SCENE

                    JAKES
          Kennedy's advisor's wanted him out of there,
          but Kennedy was reluctant to do anything.

FLASHBACK B/W

**IN THE WHITE HOUSE OVAL OFFICE an AIDE drops a
"Washington Post" on the President's desk. The front page is**

dominated by a PHOTO of a Buddhist monk burning serenely in the street.

> JAKES (V.O.)
> Then the monks started setting themselves on
> fire...

PRESIDENT KENNEDY picks up the paper and sits back, shaken.

> JAKES (V.O.)
> And Kennedy knew we could never win with
> Diem in power.

BACK TO SCENE

Jakes looks into the distance.

> JAKES
> Somehow, I got tapped to oversee a coup.

FLASHBACK B/W

IN ARVN STAFF OFFICES high-ranking ARVN officers engage in serious conversation. GENERAL TONG is among them.

> JAKES (V.O.)
> There were plots and counter plots rumored
> every day, and no shortage of generals who
> wanted Diem out. But Diem still had pockets
> of support in the military and wasn't going to
> go quietly. It was important to have the right
> generals in charge. We wanted as little
> bloodshed as possible.

ON THE NIGHT OF THE COUP the rebellious generals conduct the battle from a command center. JAKES hovers on the fringes.

> JAKES (V.O.)
> On the night of the coup I was with Tong and
> the other generals. I wasn't supposed to be
> anywhere near the place, but I didn't trust
> them.

IN THE PRESIDENTIAL PALACE two men hurry through an underground escape tunnel and emerge onto a deserted side street. It is PRESIDENT DIEM and his brother NHU. GUNFIRE and EXPLOSIONS rattle the night. A nondescript sedan awaits.

> JAKES (V.O.)
> When the palace fell, Diem and Nhu fled to a
> Catholic church in Cholon.

IN A CATHOLIC CHURCH, hands shaking, NHU dials the phone and hands it to DIEM.

> JAKES (V.O.)
> Later, when he knew all was lost, Diem called
> the generals to negotiate his surrender.

IN ARVN STAFF OFFICES an ARVN General takes the phone.

INTERCUT DIEM/ARVN GENERAL as they talk. Diem is haggard, confused—a flawed character caught in a tragic web.

> JAKES (V.O.)
> Diem agreed to step down, asking only for safe
> passage out of the country. I'd already
> arranged transport. Looked like things were
> working out.

BACK TO SCENE

Jakes looks out over the ocean.

> JAKES
> There was still fighting in the city, so Tong was
> assigned to pick them up and get them safely to
> the air base.

FLASHBACK B/W

ON THE STREETS OF SAIGON a convoy of trucks and armored personnel carriers (APCs) bristling with ARVN soldiers stops near a Catholic church. DIEM and NHU emerge. GENERAL TONG greets them politely and gestures to an APC.

JAKES (V.O.)

But Tong had his own ideas. Seems he had a
grudge against Diem for some past business.

As Diem and Nhu disappear into the vehicle, Tong flashes a hard look to MAJOR CHINH, a sadistic-looking fellow, and holds up two fingers. Chinh and an ARVN CAPTAIN with a submachine gun climb in with Diem. The convoy moves off.

INSIDE THE APC Diem chats nervously. Nhu is subdued and wary. The ARVN officers sit stone-faced.

THE CONVOY stops for no reason. In his truck, General Tong lights a cigar, waiting.

INSIDE THE APC the ARVN officers OPEN FIRE on Diem and Nhu, emptying their weapons into the twitching bodies.

GENERAL TONG puffs his cigar as he listens.

INSIDE THE APC Major Chinh runs out of ammo. He pulls a knife and repeatedly stabs Diem and Nhu's lifeless bodies until finally he stops, breathing hard, covered with blood.

GENERAL TONG gestures to his driver. The convoy moves off.

BACK TO SCENE

Noone and Jakes sit in silence.

JAKES

They said when Kennedy was told about Diem
he turned white as a ghost. Had to leave the
room. Three weeks later, *he* was assassinated.

IN SUONG LE'S BEDROOM AT NIGHT

SUONG LE does homework in a simply furnished room with books and record albums. She has trouble concentrating, her expression suggesting thoughts of her encounter with Noone. She hears something and glances to a curtained DOORWAY.

IN MADAME YEN'S BEDROOM

MADAME YEN drops a few things, then sits before a dressing table mirror. It is a richly furnished room of Chinese and French antiques. She picks up a hairbrush and sets it down without using it, making a distinctive sound. After a moment she does it again.

SUONG LE glides through the curtained doorway. She takes hairpins from Madame Yen's hair and lets it fall, then begins brushing. [*Dialogue in French, subtitles*]

> MADAME YEN
> The American tonight, Sergeant Noone. What
> did he say?

> SUONG LE
> (trying the sound)
> Sergeant Noone...

> MADAME YEN
> What did he say?

> SUONG LE
> Nothing much.

> MADAME YEN
> He asked to see you?

> SUONG LE
> In a way...

> MADAME YEN
> You told him no?

Suong Le brushes without speaking.

> MADAME YEN
> You told him no?

> SUONG LE
> You know I think of men sometimes. What it
> would be like.

                    MADAME YEN
Forget him.

                    SUONG LE
He is no one.

                    MADAME YEN
You are forbidden to see him.

                    SUONG LE
                 (gathering courage)
Tet is not far away. You said when I was
nineteen —

                    MADAME YEN
Not him!

                    SUONG LE
I'm only curious.

Madame Yen stands to face her.

                    MADAME YEN
Only curious…

                    SUONG LE
Yes, what it would be like.

Madame Yen strokes Suong Le's hair.

                    MADAME YEN
So dangerous.

                    SUONG LE
There is no danger.

                    MADAME YEN
With men there is always danger.

                    SUONG LE
I can take care of myself.

MADAME YEN
Love makes you helpless.

SUONG LE
I feel nothing for him.

Madame Yen slides Suong Le's robe from her shoulders. It falls to the floor. Suong Le stands naked, beautiful.

MADAME YEN
We both know that's not true.

Madame Yen slides a slow finger across Suong Le's breast.

SUONG LE
(eyes lowered)
I would not leave you.

ON THE STREET OUTSIDE CLUB PARIS IN DAYLIGHT

Sidewalk tables stand empty, except one, at which sits MADAME YEN. She glances at her watch as NOONE approaches.

MADAME YEN
You come at the right time — a good quality in a
man.

NOONE
Suong Le's not joining us?

MADAME YEN
She has school.

NOONE
I wanted to tell her how much I enjoyed her
singing.

MADAME YEN
You told her quite a lot last night. How could
you have left that out?

                    NOONE
We barely spoke.

                    MADAME YEN
Yet much was said.

The BARTENDER, waiting nearby, approaches.

                    BARTENDER
Scotch, sir? Something old and expensive?

They exchange grins.

                    NOONE
You're the boss.

                    MADAME YEN
Bring a new bottle.

The bartender hurries off.

                    NOONE
Club Paris is an extraordinary place.

                    MADAME YEN
An inheritance. The man who owned it died
while I was married to him.

                    NOONE
While or because?

Madame Yen smiles. The bartender brings Noone's scotch and pours
the first drink. Noone examines the label, impressed.

                    NOONE
Twenty-five years...
        (sips)
Well worth the wait.

                    MADAME YEN
Take it with you. My gift.

Noone raises his glass to her in thanks. Madame Yen dismisses the bartender with a nod.

                    MADAME YEN
          Do you know what you are doing?

                    NOONE
          How do you mean?

                    MADAME YEN
          What role you will play — in our business.

                    NOONE
          Do what Jakes asks, I guess.

                    MADAME YEN
          And what his partner asks?

                    NOONE
          I doubt you're in my chain-of-command.

                    MADAME YEN
              (alluring smile)
          That remains to be seen.

With a nod from Madame Yen, street VENDORS approach with food from steaming carts. They carefully arrange bowls of rice, fruit, soup, platters of fish and colorful vegetables, baskets of steamed snails. The table is a work of art.

                    NOONE
              (to vendors, Vietnamese)
          It's beautiful.

Madame Yen nods her approval. The vendors bow and leave.

                    NOONE
          All this food...

With Geisha-like precision, she freshens Noone's drink. Heavy pour.

MADAME YEN
(in French)
I hope you are a man of strong appetite.

NOONE
My French is rusty.

MADAME YEN
Too bad. It's the language of love.

IN A CATHOLIC GIRLS' SCHOOL IN VIETNAM

SUONG LE daydreams out the window as the teacher drones on.
The teacher calls her name, startling her. Girls titter.

ON THE STREET OUTSIDE CLUB PARIS

NOONE and MADAME YEN finish lunch. She glances at her watch
as she delicately wipes her mouth. Noone moves to leave.

NOONE
Lunch was excellent. Thank you.

Madame Yen freshens his drink.

MADAME YEN
I asked because you remind me of someone.

NOONE
Friend or foe?

MADAME YEN
Someone I was in love with.

NOONE
That could go either way.

Madame Yen stands and picks up the bottle of scotch.

MADAME YEN
Come. I'll show you his picture.

She takes a few steps, then looks back over her shoulder. Noone
hesitates, then stands.

                         MADAME YEN
          Bring your drink.

When they've gone, street CHILDREN appear from nowhere and
hurriedly eat what's been left on the table.

OUTSIDE THE CATHOLIC GIRLS' SCHOOL

SUONG LE emerges from the building, talking and laughing with
other girls. She hails a cyclo and climbs in. As she rides, her private
smile suggests, perhaps, thoughts of Noone.

SUONG LE'S P.O.V as she gazes at the people she passes. Each
FACE holds a story...

IN MADAME YEN'S APARTMENT

NOONE looks around, sipping scotch.

                         NOONE
          You have beautiful things.

                         MADAME YEN (O.S.)
          His picture is in here.

Noone goes into her bedroom. He knows better than to be here, but
is a moth to the flame. MADAME YEN is behind a dressing screen.

                         MADAME YEN (O.S.)
          In the nightstand drawer.

Noone looks at it. The photo is of Madame Yen at 18, arm in arm
with a French soldier.

                         NOONE
          We don't look anything alike.

                    MADAME YEN (O.S.)
     I did not say you looked alike. Only that you
     remind me.

                    NOONE
     He was killed?

                    MADAME YEN (O.S.)
     Worse. He went home and got married. Even
     wrote to tell me.

                    NOONE
     Thoughtful.

                    MADAME YEN (O.S.)
     My father was also a French soldier. My mother
     never knew which one.

She emerges from behind the screen in a silk robe.

                    MADAME YEN
     As a child she taught me what men like... and
     what I like. I watched her make love from
     behind a curtain.

She seems transformed. Soft, demure, almost in imitation of Suong
Le and of her eighteen-year-old self in the picture.

                    MADAME YEN
     I followed her way when I was twelve.

Her robe is slightly open. She wears nothing underneath.

                    NOONE
     Look, I think —

                    MADAME YEN
     I called myself a courtesan and soon had only
     rich men for lovers.

She steps close and touches his hand.

                    NOONE
          It's not that I don't—

                 MADAME YEN
          Do you know why?

Noone can't help being drawn in.

                    NOONE
          Because you're beautiful?

She brings his hand to her lips.

                 MADAME YEN
          Because I studied the art of love and became
          an artist.

She places his hand between her legs and holds it there.

                 MADAME YEN
          And because I know things...

ON THE STREET OUTSIDE CLUB PARIS

A cyclo pulls up. SUONG LE climbs out and pays the driver.

IN SUONG LE'S BEDROOM

SUONG LE drops her books on the bed with casual habit and quickly
slips out of her white *ao dai* to change. Underneath, she is wearing
not much.

Suddenly, the soft MOAN of a woman O.S. Suong Le looks towards
the curtain to Madame Yen's room. She hesitates, then goes to it,
catching a glimpse of LOVERS.

She looks quickly away, then is drawn to look again. Through an
opening in the curtain she sees Madame Yen making love with a
man. She turns away, then back. She watches, intrigued.

The lovers change position and she sees the man is NOONE. She
gasps and turns away. After a moment, she is drawn again to look.
76

INTERCUT SUONG LE/LOVERS

Suong Le watches the softly erotic lovemaking between the man she desires and the only lover she's known. Her hand slides to her breast, lingers, then moves lower...

Her face is radiant. Her eyelids flutter, lips part... There is a small, sharp intake of breath.

IN THE SKY OVER JUNGLE MOUNTAINS

Sudden SOUND OF ENGINES as a black Caribou cargo plane is silhouetted by sunrise.

INSIDE the plane, NOONE, COBB and JAKES sit among crates of weapons, playing pinochle. Jakes looks at Noone.

                    JAKES
          You did good with that chief yesterday. What
          you said made a difference.

Noone nods.

                    JAKES
          This is it, though. Doesn't matter who else we
          got. If Y-Bham's not in, it ain't happening.

                    COBB
               (winks at Noone)
          I believe you've mentioned that.

Jakes seems almost nervous. There is much at stake.

                    JAKES
          Can't be said enough. Getting these other chiefs
          and militias just helps make our case to Y-Bham.
          This is the ballgame right here.

IN A JUNGLE CLEARING IN CAMBODIA

The plane touches down on a bumpy dirt runway. FULRO SOLDIERS unload the cargo.

IN A HMONG VILLAGE IN CAMBODIA

The Americans are led past several longhouses to one slightly bigger
and more elaborate than the others. They climb the steps.

INSIDE is an efficient military office. FULRO soldiers in fatigues look
up from what they're doing and smile.

GENERAL Y-BHAM ENUOL, commanding officer of FULRO, rises
from his desk to greet them — sincere face, old-world manners. He
speaks English with a French accent.

> Y-BHAM ENOUL
> Mister Jakes.

> JAKES
> General. You know Sergeant Cobb.

> COBB
> General.

> JAKES
> And this is Sergeant Noone.

> NOONE
> It's an honor to meet you, General.

> Y-BHAM ENOUL
> And you, Sergeant.

> NOONE
> I read the transcript of your address to the '64
> conference at Phnom Penh.

Y-Bham is surprised, impressed. So is Jakes.

> NOONE
> A very powerful speech.

> Y-BHAM
> That accomplished very little.

                          NOONE
          It takes more than words to stop genocide.

Y-Bham regards Noone for a long moment.

                          Y-BHAM
          Yes. So very much more.

IN THE HMONG VILLAGE

Pigs and chickens wander, women cook, children play, old men
squat on their heels smoking pipes. A young mother nurses twins.
Two boys play guns with sticks. Two soldiers load weapons onto an
ELEPHANT.

Under an open shelter Y-BHAM and the AMERICANS share food
and sip rice wine from common jars, along with FULRO OFFICERS
and village ELDERS. Hmong girls serve them and add water to the
wine jars as needed. One of them feeds Y-GAR, an elder with
gnarled, useless hands.

                          JAKES
          There are many more weapons coming.

                       Y-BHAM ENOUL
          We are grateful, of course.

                          JAKES
          And we can offer more Special Forces to train
          your men.

Y-Bham nods thanks.

                          JAKES
          As many as you need.

Y-Bham takes a bite of food and chews slowly, then sips rice wine
from the nearest jar. Jakes shifts position slightly.

                       Y-BHAM ENOUL
          Things have been happening rather fast lately,
          Mister Jakes. I must ask myself, "Why?"

                    JAKES
                 (deep breath)
There's a new American strategy for the
Highlands.

                Y-BHAM ENOUL
Strategy...

                    JAKES
My government now looks favorably on the
idea of a sovereign Hmong nation as a buffer
between two Vietnams.

                Y-BHAM ENOUL
Looks favorably...

                    JAKES
The CIA is prepared to support and assist an
uprising in the Highlands. If successful, my
government would immediately recognize your
sovereignty and sign a mutual defense treaty.

                Y-BHAM ENOUL
And Saigon?

                    JAKES
We are working to minimize resistance.

                Y-BHAM ENOUL
It is our dream, of course.

                    JAKES
The new nation must seal off NVA infiltration
through Laos and Cambodia. With our help.

                Y-BHAM ENOUL
When the Hmong are finally united that would
be no problem.

                    JAKES
There is some urgency.

                    Y-BHAM ENOUL
          We can be ready in perhaps a year.

                       JAKES
          In six months it may be too late.

                    Y-BHAM ENOUL
          We must also be prepared to govern.

                       JAKES
          The war is at a critical juncture.

Y-Bham shakes his head.

                    Y-BHAM ENOUL
          If we move too soon and fail...

                       JAKES
          It's worth the risk.

                    Y-BHAM ENOUL
                   (sudden intensity)
          You risk nothing! We risk everything!

No one speaks as Y-Bham deliberates. He appears on the verge of
rejecting it. Jakes shifts position. It seems about to fall apart...

                       NOONE
                    (in Rhade)
          The risk of action is great, but the risk of no
          action may be greater.

Surprised, Y-Bham looks at Noone.

                       NOONE
                    (in English)
          How long will this opportunity remain? The ebb
          and flow of war... Will an alliance of this
          magnitude be offered twice? There may be
          wisdom in not saying "No" too quickly.

Y-Bham considers in silence, then turns to Y-GAR.

> Y-BHAM ENOUL
> (in Rhade)
> Old friend, they ask us to risk everything on the
> promises of America. What words can you offer?

As Y-Gar responds, Cobb translates for Jakes.

> Y-GAR/COBB
> (long pause)
> In the year we ate the forest of the spirit Baa Ko...

FLASHBACK B/W

YEARS BEFORE IN Y-GAR'S VILLAGE, Viet Cong (VC) soldiers harass villagers. A VC CAPTAIN talks heatedly to Y-GAR, who is apparently village chief.

> **Y-GAR/COBB (V.O.)**
> **Communist soldiers come to our village. They
> say, "Give us food and young men."**

Y-Gar argues with the VC captain, gesturing with strong hands.

> **Y-GAR/COBB (V.O.)**
> **We say we have barely enough food to feed
> our children.**

The VC captain nods and two VC soldiers grab Y-Gar to restrain him. Two others drag his PREGNANT WIFE from her hut as their young DAUGHTER flails at them with small fists. A VC soldier cracks the child's head with the butt of his rifle. She crumples.

> **Y-GAR/COBB (V.O.)**
> **So they drag my wife from our house...**

Y-Gar's wife is held by VC soldiers. The VC Captain approaches with a machete.

> **Y-GAR/COBB (V.O.)**
> **They cut open her fat belly...**

The VC Captain slides the machete across her stomach as an anguished Y-Gar strains against his captors.

> **Y-GAR/COBB (V.O.)**
> Her child and entrails spill to the earth.

BACK TO SCENE

The Americans are visibly moved.

> Y-GAR/COBB
> They took food and young men. Who could stop them?

Y-Gar gestures with scarred, twisted hands.

> Y-GAR/COBB
> Then government soldiers came.

FLASHBACK B/W

IN Y-GAR'S VILLAGE it is now **ARVN** soldiers who bully villagers and interrogate elders, including **Y-GAR**.

> **Y-GAR/COBB (V.O.)**
> They call us enemy for giving food and young
> men to the communists.

Y-Gar is beaten by several **ARVN** soldiers and dragged to a cooking fire. They push his hands into the **COALS**.

> **Y-GAR/COBB (V.O.)**
> They hold our arms in fire.

BACK TO SCENE

The Americans are strongly affected by his words.

> Y-GAR/COBB
> Now the Americans offer their hand. We take it
> because we have no other friends.

Y-GAR looks at Jakes.

> Y-GAR/COBB
> Will they stand by us? No one knows. If yes, our
> children may know their grandchildren. If no,
> we will be hunted and killed by the Indochine
> until not even the trees will remember our
> passing.

Y-BHAM looks in the eyes of each American as he deliberates.

> Y-BHAM ENOUL
> We will move when you say it is time.

IN A CITY IN VIETNAM

NOONE sits alone in his parked jeep, looking down the block to
Club Paris. SUONG LE emerges in white *ao dai* and straw hat, school
books cradled in her arms. She hails a cyclo. Noone starts his jeep
and follows slowly at a distance.

AT A CATHOLIC GIRLS' SCHOOL Suong Le climbs out of the cyclo
and is greeted by other girls dressed similarly, holding books.
Vietnamese NUNS talk nearby. Suong Le goes inside.

NOONE pulls up to the school. A pretty COLLEGE GIRL approaches
with a gleam in her eye.

> NOONE
> (in Vietnamese)
> What time does school get out?

> COLLEGE GIRL
> (in English)
> Two-thirty. You give me ride home?

> NOONE
> Some other time.

> COLLEGE GIRL
> I make you very happy.

                              NOONE
          Some other time.

He drives off. A NUN approaches. [*Dialogue in Vietnamese*]

                               NUN
          This is college, not a G.I. bar.

                          COLLEGE GIRL
                            (saucy)
          How do you think I pay for school?

NOONE drives aimlessly, lost in thought. He takes in the passing
FACES, each telling a story...

A BUDDHIST TEMPLE appears. Noone is drawn to it.

INSIDE THE BUDDHIST TEMPLE

NOONE looks around, then stops in front of a Buddha statue and
stares at it. Buddha stares back...

NOONE'S P.O.V. as the SCENE VIBRATES, reminiscent of the
transcendental state that overcame him in the jungle...

NOONE stares transfixed at the Buddha, tears flowing.

                           DAO (O.S.)
                          (in English)
          Welcome.

Noone turns to see DAO, the monk from the opening sequence. His
smile radiates wisdom and compassion. Noone wipes his eyes.

                               DAO
          Crying is allowed.

                              NOONE
          I don't know what's happening to me.

                               DAO
          You are in the right place. Come.

Dao leads Noone into a back room with pillows on the floor. They sit.

                    NOONE
          What do I do?

                    DAO
          You are doing it.

They sit in silence. On one wall is a MAP of Southeast Asia. Drawn on it is a YIN-YANG SYMBOL in perfect attunement with the geography of Vietnam. Dao sees Noone's eyes are drawn to it.

                    DAO
          From the interplay of opposites, all possibilities
          arise.

                    NOONE
          It fits the map so perfectly.

                    DAO
          Drawn by my master, the night before he
          entered the fire.

                    NOONE
          Entered the fire?

                    DAO
          Burned in the street. He was the first. Very
          famous now.

                    NOONE
          I've seen the picture.

                    DAO
          He believed this time and place is a spiritual
          door... if one is ripe.

                    NOONE
          Ripe?

                    DAO
          A person ready to let go. A fruit ready to drop.

                    NOONE
          Drop into what?

                    DAO
          Truth.

                    NOONE
               (slightly mocking)
          Secrets of the universe?

                    DAO
          No secrets. Truth is before your eyes, always.

This strikes a chord.

                    NOONE
          Hidden in plain sight...

                    DAO
          Yes.

Noone stares at his hands.

                    NOONE
          I was given a glimpse, but it's gone.

                    DAO
          It never leaves. It is who you are.

                    NOONE
          Nothing seems real anymore.

                    DAO
          You are on the edge. Remain there and
          something may happen.

                    NOONE
          I don't understand.

                    DAO
          Understanding is not necessary.

                    NOONE
I don't know what to do.

                    DAO
Without hope or fear watch your life unfold.
Nothing else is required.

IN MADAME YEN'S OFFICE

MADAME YEN presides from behind an antique French desk.
Seated across from her is CADEO, her main hood. Two other
HOODS sit nearby. [*Dialogue in Vietnamese*]

                    CADEO
We lost two more distributors. Tong's power is
increasing fast.

                    HOOD 1
His heroin operation generates huge profits. He
can offer better deals.

                    HOOD 2
He'll bury us if we don't keep up.

                    CADEO
We need to make heroin.

                    MADAME YEN
I'm not in that business.

                    CADEO
It is the future.

                    MADAME YEN
I'm old-fashioned.

                    CADEO
Well, if something isn't done soon he'll be
fucking us all in the ass!

Madame Yen, not pleased by the outburst, considers.

                         MADAME YEN
                Find the location of his factory.

                          CADEO
                That's impossible! Only his closest—

                         MADAME YEN
                Find it!

IN AN ARVN MILITARY COMPOUND

A JEEP is waived through the gate, JAKES driving.

IN GENERAL TONG'S STAFF OFFICES

Several ARVN SOLDIERS work at desks. Presiding over the office is
MAJOR CHINH, President Diem's assassin. Jakes strolls in. Major
Chinh picks up a phone.

                         MAJOR CHINH
                       (in Vietnamese)
                Jakes is here.

Jakes surrenders his handgun and allows himself to be frisked by
two GUARDS standing outside an impressive door.

IN GENERAL TONG'S OFFICE

GENERAL TONG sits behind a massive desk in an impeccably
tailored dress uniform. The room is large, well appointed, more
opulent than one might expect for a military office—tall oriental
VASES on pedestals, antique SWORDS on the walls. JAKES enters.

                         GENERAL TONG
                Mister Jakes. Thank you for coming.

Jakes walks the room.

                          JAKES
                Nice place you got here.

GENERAL TONG

I generally don't like to do business in this
office, but for you I make an exception. Cuban?

Jakes takes several and slips them into his pocket. Tong takes out two
more, then steps to an array of antique SWORDS and slides the tip of
a cigar across an EDGE. Razor sharp, it cuts the tip clean.

GENERAL TONG
(handing Jakes the cigar)
Smoke with me. I have a proposal I think will be
of great interest.

Tong slices off the tip of the other cigar on a different sword.

GENERAL TONG

It involves your good friend General Y-Bham
Enuol.

Jakes becomes wary.

GENERAL TONG

I know how important the Montagnards are to
the American strategy...

Tong holds a lighter for their cigars.

JAKES

And to Saigon's as well.

GENERAL TONG

Yes, of course. Still, it seems you have a unique
interest, Mister Jakes.

JAKES

I do what's in the best interests of both our
governments.

GENERAL TONG

As do we all.

                    JAKES
Where is this going?

                    GENERAL TONG
Suppose the Hmong were to stage another
uprising — try to regain their sovereignty...

Jakes remains impassive.

                    GENERAL TONG
A lot of bloodshed could be avoided if my
planes never left the ground.

The import of his words hits Jakes.

                    JAKES
You'd let a revolution succeed?

                    GENERAL TONG
I'm a businessman not a politician.

                    JAKES
Or a loyalist, as we well know.

Tong lets it slide.

                    GENERAL TONG
In an emerging Hmong nation a man in your
position would have great influence. Enough to
grant exclusive opium rights.

                    JAKES
You overestimate me.

                    GENERAL TONG
I don't think so.

                    JAKES
An interesting hypothetical, but —

GENERAL TONG
I will pay twice what you get from Madame Yen
for all your shipments now. And if this situation
with the Montagnards should arise...

Jakes says nothing. After a few moments he stands to leave.

GENERAL TONG
Think it over, Mister Jakes, but don't take too
long. Things are moving fast.

ON THE STREET OUTSIDE SUONG LE'S SCHOOL

NOONE watches from his jeep as GIRLS leave. They all look
beautiful and similar—black hair, white *ao dais*, conical straw hats.
Yet when SUONG LE appears she stands out. Her grace and beauty
are a thing apart. Noone pulls up beside her.

NOONE
Hello.

Surprised and flustered to see him, she walks away up the street. He
drives slowly alongside.

SUONG LE
You startled me.

NOONE
I'm sorry.

SUONG LE
Why are you here?

NOONE
Such a complex question.

SUONG LE
At my school.

NOONE
I was in the neighborhood.

He stops the jeep. She hesitates, then climbs in.

ON A BEACH IN VIETNAM

SUONG LE and NOONE walk white sand between palms and surf.

> NOONE
> Do you like college?

> SUONG LE
> Mostly. Sometimes I've had enough of books.

> NOONE
> You were born a Catholic?

> SUONG LE
> Yes.

> NOONE
> And you believe in it?

> SUONG LE
> Why wouldn't I? Everyone needs to believe
> something, don't they?

> NOONE
> I don't know. I suppose.

> SUONG LE
> What do you believe in?

> NOONE
> That's kind of up in the air right now.
> (looks at her)
> Love, maybe.

Their eyes lock.

> SUONG LE
> We should not be doing this. Madame Yen—

NOONE

You are with her by choice?

SUONG LE
(hesitates)

No.

NOONE

Then why?

SUONG LE

It is difficult to explain.

NOONE

I have time.

SUONG LE
(eyes lowered)

I am owned.

NOONE

No one owns anybody.

SUONG LE

You don't know her.

NOONE

I know enough.

SUONG LE

Some might say too much.

NOONE

You're incredibly beautiful. You know that,
don't you?

SUONG LE

More beautiful than Madame Yen?

Noone picks up a perfect SEASHELL and hands it to her.

                    NOONE
More beautiful than anyone.

Suong Le gazes at the shell.

                    SUONG LE
My room is next to hers. I saw you with her.

                    NOONE
Suong Le, I—

                    SUONG LE
I am only stating a fact—that I saw you. Like
saying I saw a red bird this morning.

                    NOONE
It was nothing.

                    SUONG LE
She would be disappointed to hear that.

                    NOONE
I was drinking—

                    SUONG LE
That's your excuse?

                    NOONE
You're jealous.

                    SUONG LE
Am I?

                    NOONE
Are you?

                    SUONG LE
Maybe a little.

                    NOONE
Of me or of her?

                    SUONG LE
           (beat)
     Of her.

Noone takes her by the shoulders.

                    NOONE
     I want to be with you.

                    SUONG LE
     That's not possible. She has claimed you.

                    NOONE
     Everything's possible.

                    SUONG LE
     If I want to experience a man it will have to be
     someone else now.

                    NOONE
     No...

He kisses her. She slaps him. They stand close. She kisses him. The
kiss deepens.

                    NOONE
     Come with me. Now.

Suong Le's hands move almost involuntarily over Noone's arms.

                    SUONG LE
     So you can make love to me then leave me alone
     to face her?

                    NOONE
     Stay with me. Never go back.

                    SUONG LE
     That's crazy.

                    NOONE
     You make me feel something I thought I'd never —

She abruptly kisses him again. Passion escalates.

                              NOONE
                    I want to take care of you.

                             SUONG LE
                   You make it sound possible.

                              NOONE
                   Say yes and it will happen.

ACT IV: ON THE STREET OUTSIDE CLUB PARIS

NOONE pulls up in his jeep with SUONG LE. She looks at him a
moment, then gets out.

IN MADAME YEN'S APARTMENT

MADAME YEN sees all from a second story window. She leaves the
window and waits as Suong Le ascends the stairs to the living room.
[*Dialogue in Vietnamese*]

                           MADAME YEN
                     Where were you?

Suong Le continues towards her room.

                             SUONG LE
                     Walking by the sea.

Madame Yen steps in front of her. They stare at each other. Suddenly
Madame Yen thrusts her hand down the front of Suong Le's pants.
Suong Le gasps as her fingers find their mark. Madame Yen
withdraws her hand and raises it to her nose.

                             SUONG LE
              No, unlike you, I have not experienced him—yet.

Madame Yen slaps her. Suong Le looks at her with submissive
defiance. Madame Yen reaches to stroke Suong Le's hair
apologetically. Suong Le turns away.

IN COLONEL HAN'S CELL

NOONE and COLONEL HAN sit smoking. They've become comfortable with each other.

                    COLONEL HAN
So now you're a Buddhist.

                    NOONE
I'm not anything. That monk knows something, though.

                    COLONEL HAN
As religions go, Buddhism is about as good as it gets, I suppose.

                    NOONE
You're not a believer?

                    COLONEL HAN
I believe that beliefs should be questioned.

                    NOONE
The examined life.

                    COLONEL HAN
Something like that.

                    NOONE
What if you don't like what you see?

                    COLONEL HAN
It's there whether you see it or not. Better to see.

                    NOONE
Some things are hard to look at.

                    COLONEL HAN
All the more reason.

                    NOONE
You're at peace with your choices?

COLONEL HAN
I've chosen to do what I could not do otherwise.

NOONE
You believe it's all destiny?

COLONEL HAN
I'm not a believer, remember?

They smoke in silence.

NOONE
You married?

COLONEL HAN
Twenty-two years. You?

NOONE
Came close once.

COLONEL HAN
And now you're thinking about it again.

NOONE
I have no clue what I'm thinking.

Colonel Han looks uncomfortable and hastens to the toilet. SOUND
of diarrhea. He returns.

NOONE
That hasn't gone away yet?

COLONEL HAN
(hesitates)
It's not something that goes away.

NOONE
What do you mean?

COLONEL HAN
I have a... condition.

NOONE

What condition? Have you seen a doctor?

COLONEL HAN

I've been to a doctor in Hanoi. I can't go to a
military doctor.

NOONE

Is it serious?

COLONEL HAN

Yes.

NOONE

Why haven't you taken care of it?

COLONEL HAN

It's not something one recovers from. The doctor
I saw says there is nothing that can be done.

NOONE

Jesus, Han...

COLONEL HAN

If the Army knows I have it I'll be discharged as
unfit for duty. If I can last another year, I'll be
eligible for a pension that my wife will continue
to receive after my death.

NOONE

A year?!

COLONEL HAN

I have made my peace with it. I just want to
make it to my pension. And until being
captured, I was hoping to see my grandchild.
Did I tell you my daughter is pregnant?

NOONE

No, you... Jesus, Han... Shit...

IN CLUB PARIS AT NIGHT

The evening is in full swing. NOONE drinks alone at the bar. He glances at Madame Yen's empty table. He orders another.

MADAME YEN enters and sits at her table. Noone joins her.

> MADAME YEN
> I enjoyed our lunch. Perhaps you'd like to come again.

> NOONE
> You arranged it so Suong Le would see us.

> MADAME YEN
> Did I?

> NOONE
> It was your only purpose.

She touches him with erotic confidence.

> MADAME YEN
> Not entirely.

> NOONE
> Look, you're an extraordinary woman—

> MADAME YEN
> Thank you.

> NOONE
> But Suong Le and I—

> MADAME YEN
> Don't say her name—

> NOONE
> We want to be together.

> MADAME YEN
> Impossible. She belongs to me.

NOONE
Let her decide.

MADAME YEN
There is nothing to decide.

NOONE
(realizing as he speaks)
I'm in love with her.

Madame Yen's eyes flare. The lights dim. MUSIC fades up.

ON STAGE the spotlight falls on SUONG LE, a white flower in her hair. She sings "Don't Explain," somehow evoking Billie Holiday while making the song uniquely her own.

SUONG LE
(singing)
Hush now, don't explain...
Just say you'll remain...
I'm glad... you're bad...
Don't explain.

As she sings she looks at Noone and Madame Yen.

SUONG LE
Fire, don't explain...
What is there to gain?...
Forget that lipstick...
Don't explain.

As before, she is mesmerizing.

SUONG LE
You know that I love you...
And what love endures...
All my thoughts are of you,
for I'm so completely yours.

Her most tender looks are for Noone. Madame Yen sees this.

                         SUONG LE
          Cry to hear folks chatter,
          and I know you cheat...
          Right or wrong don't matter,
          when you're with me sweet.

Noone's eyes are riveted on Suong Le.

                         SUONG LE
          Hush now, don't explain...
          You're my joy and pain...
          My life, is yours love...
          Don't explain.

SUONG LE bows to enthusiastic APPLAUSE. She steps off stage and
joins Noone and Madame Yen. The threesome sit without speaking.
So many ways it could go from here...

Madame Yen gestures to two BOUNCERS.

                       MADAME YEN
          Sergeant Noone is leaving. He is never to be let
          back in.

The bouncers lays hands on Noone.

                         SUONG LE
          No!

Noone stands abruptly and WHACKS the shit out of both of them,
then pulls a GUN. The music stops. All eyes turn towards Noone.

                          NOONE
                       (to Suong Le)
          Come with me.

Suong Le looks like she might.

                       MADAME YEN
                       (in French)
          He will leave you.

                    NOONE
Come with me now.

The bouncers get up and are reinforced by CADEO and HOODS
with GUNS. Madame Yen stares intently at Suong Le.

                  MADAME YEN
                  (in French)
He will go home without you — or perhaps,
die here. So many ways a soldier can die…

Suong Le understands her meaning. She looks at Noone.

                  SUONG LE
            (reluctant but convincing)
I choose to stay. Please do not come back.

Cadeo eyeballs Noone as he stares at Suong Le. Suong Le lowers her
eyes. Reluctantly accepting the futility of the situation, Noone pushes
past the hoods to leave.

As he does he sees JAKES — who has just entered and caught the last
few moments of the scene — staring a hole through him from across
the room. Noone storms out the door.

ON THE STREET OUTSIDE CLUB PARIS

JAKES catches up to NOONE.

                    JAKES
              (livid astonishment)
What the fuck did I just see?!

                    NOONE
I fucked up.

                    JAKES
Fucked up? Fucked up?! You just put the whole
operation in jeopardy!

                    NOONE
Things got out of hand. I'm sorry.

JAKES
What the fuck did you do?

NOONE
(deep breath)
I told Madame Yen I was in love with Suong Le.

JAKES
Unbelievable. Did you fuck her?

NOONE
Who?

JAKES
Who?! Suong Le!

NOONE
No...

JAKES
(hits him)
Linh?! You fucked Madame Yen?!

NOONE
Sort of.

JAKES
Sort of?! Jesus Christ there's no way you could
have screwed up more if you planned it!

NOONE
Things have been strange lately.

JAKES
It's almost fucking comical.

NOONE
I'm really sorry.

Jakes settles down and appears to soften.

                    JAKES
                (snorts a laugh)
           Jesus, Noone. I mean, Jesus!

                    NOONE
           I'd fix it if I could.

                    JAKES
           No! You've done enough. I'll take care of the
           fixing. Linh needs me as much as I need her. Just
           stay away from both of them. Got it?

                    NOONE
           Seems that won't be a problem.

They stand in silence as Jakes comes full circle.

                    JAKES
           You're a good man, Noone. I'm not sure we'd be
           where we are without you. This doesn't change
           anything.

                    NOONE
           Thank you.

                    JAKES
           Shit. We could both use a break. Might be a
           good time to visit that little village. What're you
           doing tomorrow?

                    NOONE
           Wide open.

IN A JUNGLE CLEARING IN LAOS

A black CARIBOU cargo plane drops onto a short, primitive runway
and brakes hard to a stop. JAKES and NOONE get out. Friendly
VILLAGERS rush to greet them.

IN A REMOTE VILLAGE IN LAOS

JAKES and NOONE drink and laugh with the jovial village CHIEF.

Attractive GIRLS wait on them. There is an innocent, "Shangri La" feel to the place.

Noone does not understand the local dialect, but Jakes knows enough to get by. He speaks to the chief, and with a look and smile, the next phase of the visit is arranged. A girl extends her hand to Noone. Another smiles at Jakes and leads them into the jungle.

After a short walk they emerge at the edge of a field. Stretched before them is an expanse of mature MARIJUANA PLANTS. Jakes examines the large, sticky buds and grins.

                    JAKES
          Most powerful shit in the Golden Triangle. In a
          league of its own.

Noone sticks his nose against a bud.

                    NOONE
          Smells fantastic.

                    JAKES
          And it's just the base for their concoction.

The girls slip out of their simple clothes and stand naked, smiling demurely for a moment, then disappear into the field.

INSIDE THE FIELD they run laughing between the plants. When they emerge they are covered with resin and a warm glow of sweat. With shards of bamboo they scrape resin from their skin and collect it in a bowl.

NOONE'S GIRL hands him her scraper with a smile and gesture. Noone slides it across her smooth brown body as she watches.

JAKES' GIRL takes a small bottle from a pouch she brought. She shakes powder from it into the bowl of resin and mixes it in.

                    NOONE
          What's that?

JAKES

Some kind of root.

NOONE

What's it called?

JAKES

Does it matter?

JAKES' GIRL produces two pipes from the pouch and fills them with
the mixture. The girls light the pipes then hand them to Jakes and
Noone...

DISSOLVE TO:

JAKES AND NOONE lay on mats in the shade, tripping. The naked
GIRLS recline next to them.

NOONE'S P.O.V. as he gazes transfixed into a heavenly display of
FRACTAL LIGHT bursting and refracting between the translucent
leaves of a LIVING EDEN...

NOONE'S GIRL gazes at him as she refills a pipe. She SPEAKS to
him in her local dialect.

NOONE
(stoned pause)
What'd she say?

Noone's girl lights the pipe, then presses her lips to his and breathes
smoke into him...

JAKES (O.S.)
It's a saying they have. "The mother of the
world sends you her love."

IN MADAME YEN'S OFFICE

MADAME YEN signs papers for the BARTENDER. As he leaves
CADEO appears in the door. [*Dialogue in Vietnamese*]

108

CADEO
I've brought you someone. He claims to have
information you want.

She nods and Cadeo ushers in QUAN, an underworld hustler.

MADAME YEN
You have something to tell me?

QUAN
I understand you are interested in the location of
Tong's factory.

MADAME YEN
And if I were?

QUAN
I would be a good person to talk to.

MADAME YEN
What would you have to say?

Quan gestures that payment should be discussed. Madame Yen
pushes paper and pen towards him. Quan writes. Madame Yen
glances at it.

MADAME YEN
If your information is accurate, I'll pay twice
that. Deceive me...

She gestures to a scowling Cadeo.

QUAN
You will not be disappointed.

IN THE 5th SFG COMMANDER'S OFFICE

COLONEL PULLMAN reads at his desk. COBB appears at the door.

COBB
You wanted to see me, Colonel?

                    PULLMAN
Sit down, Frank.

                    COBB
What's this about?

                    PULLMAN
One of those good news, bad news things.

                    COBB
Let's have it.

Pullman hands him papers.

                    COBB
Orders?

                    PULLMAN
New rule came down from Westmoreland.
There's a hard limit on how long anybody can
stay in country.

                    COBB
And I'm fucking past it.

                    PULLMAN
You're going back stateside.

                    COBB
What's the good news.

                    PULLMAN
You're being promoted to Sergeant Major. New
Top for the 7th at Bragg.

                    COBB
Shit.

                    PULLMAN
There's nothing I can do, Frank. If there were I'd
do it.

IN THE CLUB PARIS SALON AT NIGHT

SUONG LE is in the middle of singing "Begin the Beguine."

                         SUONG LE
                          (singing)
          A moment's divine what rapture serene... Then
          clouds came along to disperse the joys we had
          tasted... And now when I hear people curse the
          chance that was wasted... I know but too well
          what they mean...

Her heart is not in it, but her indifference lends a certain pathos to
her performance.

                         SUONG LE
          So don't let them begin the beguine... Let the
          love that was once a fire remain an ember...
          Let it sleep like the dead desire I only
          remember... When they begin the beguine.

She is not the sultry chanteuse the patrons have come to know,
though, and their applause is subdued as she leaves stage to join
MADAME YEN at her table. [*Dialogue in Vietnamese*]

                         MADAME YEN
          You've sung better.

                         SUONG LE
          I'm not feeling well.

The real problem is no secret.

                         MADAME YEN
          I'm sorry about Noone, but it's for the best.

                         SUONG LE
          Best for who?

                         MADAME YEN
          You may choose another man, anyone. My gift
          for Tet.

                    SUONG LE
          I don't want your fucking gifts.

                    MADAME YEN
          Do not speak to me that way!

                    SUONG LE
                 (standing abruptly)
          I have schoolwork.

                    MADAME YEN
          I did not say you could leave.

                    SUONG LE
          May I do my schoolwork?

                    MADAME YEN
                 (beat)
          Yes.

Madame Yen reaches to touch her, but she's gone.

IN THE COURTYARD GARDEN OF THE BUDDHIST TEMPLE

A lizard crawls the garden wall. A bird sings. NOONE sits
motionless, eyes closed. DAO sits nearby. Noone opens his eyes.

                    NOONE
          Is it hard living life as a monk?

                    DAO
          Living any life is hard.

                    NOONE
          I'm a stranger to myself. It's not me watching
          life through these eyes.

                    DAO
          You are seeing clearly.

They sit in silence for a moment.

112

NOONE

It seems I'm in love.

DAO

It is sometimes described that way.

NOONE

I mean... with a woman.

DAO

(laughs)
That I cannot help you with.

NOONE

And my job, it's... I don't know. I'm being pulled
in all directions.

DAO

In a realm of no dimension, direction is
meaningless.

NOONE

I want what you have.

DAO

I have nothing.

NOONE

You have peace. You're content.

DAO

Looks deceive.

NOONE

You're not at peace?

DAO

(after a long silence)
I resolved to follow my master and enter the
fire. When the time came I hesitated. My resolve
returned, but the time had passed.

                              NOONE
          Your death was not necessary. Diem was
          deposed. The goal was achieved without it.

                              DAO
          My destiny was to enter the fire. There is no
          peace for one who refuses destiny.

IN THE MIKE FORCE TEAMHOUSE AT NIGHT

It's an ordinary evening. SF SOLDIERS and young Vietnamese
WOMEN drink, talk, play pool. "Combat" is on TV.

NOONE drifts behind the small bar and freshens his drink. Marty
walks up and sets his empty glass on the bar.

                              MARTY
          Gimmee a Beam rocks while you're back there
          will ya?

                              NOONE
                        (pouring Marty's drink)
          New club's coming along good. Ought to name
          it after you: "Big Marty's."

                              MARTY
          No thanks. Shit only gets named for you when
          you croak.

                              NOONE
          You seen Cobb?

                              MARTY
          He was at the Hilton earlier.

CAPTAIN MONROE, slightly drunk, takes a seat at the bar and
pushes his empty glass towards Noone.

                              MONROE
          You barkeep tonight?

                              NOONE
          Until I ain't. What can I get you?

                              MONROE
          Rye.

                              NOONE
          Rocks?

                              MONROE
          Neat.

Noone pours his drink and leaves the bottle on the bar. Monroe adds
more to his glass.

                              MONROE
          So, you got yourself a nice little gig with the
          Agency now.

                              NOONE
          Kinda fell in my lap.

                              MONROE
          Everything comes easy for you, don't it?

Marty shoots Noone a cautionary look and moves off.

                              NOONE
          I don't know. Sometimes…

                              MONROE
          I wanted that job. Got Cobb to get me an
          interview with Jakes. Turned me down.

                              NOONE
          I hear he prefers working with NCOs.

                              MONROE
          Yeah, what the fuck's that all about. I'm as
          fucking SF as any goddamn NCO. You know
          how long I've been in grade?

                    NOONE

No, sir. I don't.

                    MONROE

Twelve years. You think I'll ever make Major?

                    NOONE

I couldn't say.

                    MONROE

Not as long as I'm in SF, I won't. It's a fucking
dead-end for officers.

                    NOONE

Yes, sir. Most of 'em move on.

                    MONROE

Not me. I'd rather be a captain in SF than a
colonel in some fucking leg outfit. I don't want
no parts of no spit-shine fucking Army.

                    NOONE

I agree with you there.

                    MONROE

Yeah, you fucking would. Goddamn E-6
hotshot, people falling all over themselves
giving you breaks.

                    NOONE

I earn my breaks.

                    MONROE

My ass, you silver spoon motherfucker.

KIM leans on the jukebox and punches up Patsy Cline, "Crazy."

                    NOONE
                  (had enough)
Look, you resent me, fine. Just keep it to
yourself. Get in my face about it again and I'll
kick your motherfucking ass, captain bars or no.

                         MONROE
You insubordinate son-of-a-bitch. I'll have you
court martialed.

                         NOONE
Fuck you.

KIM, oblivious to their conversation, glides behind the bar and
drapes an arm over Noone.

                          KIM
                      (pouting)
Dance with me.

Noone and Monroe stare at each other without blinking. Monroe
breaks it by taking a drink. Kim tugs petulantly at Noone's arm.

                          KIM
Dance...

Kim pulls him away and holds tight as they slow dance in place.

                          KIM
What's the matter with you these day?

                         NOONE
Nothing.

                          KIM
You don't fuck me same.

                         NOONE
There's a lot going on.

                          KIM
Maybe you don't like me anymore.

                         NOONE
You're a beautiful woman.

                          KIM
Maybe you fucking somebody else.

                              NOONE
                    (beat)
          No.

She pulls him tighter. As the song ends, STILES calls out from the
pool table across the room.

                             STILES
          Noone. Need a partner for nine-ball.

Noone goes to the table and picks up a cue.

                            RENFROW
          Your break.

Noone breaks, something drops. He takes a pull at his drink and
lines up another shot.

IN THE MIKE FORCE COMPOUND AT NIGHT

NOONE emerges from the teamhouse slightly unsteady. In the
background, SF soldiers do cannonballs into a SWIMMING POOL.
He lights a smoke and looks up as he walks.

NOONE'S P.O.V. as a universe of STARS looks down...

HMONG STRIKERS sit outside rough wood barracks smoking pipes,
hand-rolled cigarettes. They smile and wave as Noone passes.

He arrives at a thatch-roof longhouse on pilings and climbs the steps.
A sign over the door reads, "Montagnard Hilton."

IN THE MONTAGNARD HILTON

STRIKERS drink beer and rice wine at mismatched tables. COBB
drinks at a table with several of them, all laughing and having a good
time, one with an arm over Cobb's shoulder.

NOONE stops at the bar to buy a half-dozen beers, then joins Cobb
and hands them around.

COBB
(drunk)
Randy fucking Noone. How the fuck are you
motherfucker?

NOONE
Jury's still out.

COBB
Tell me about it.

BAAP CANH appears with a bottle of rice wine and glasses.

NOONE
Baap Canh! Sitcha ass down.

COBB
Who's this?

BAAP CANH
I am Baap Canh.

NOONE
Tell him the whole thing.

BAAP CANH
I am called "Baap Canh No-Village."

COBB
No Village?

BAAP CANH
I have no home in this world.

NOONE
Is that beautiful or what?

COBB
Well, where were you born?

BAAP CANH
I don't remember being born.

                    COBB
          (laughs)
     I love this guy!

                   NOONE
     Used to be a shaman.

                    COBB
     No shit?

                 BAAP CANH
     Maybe again. They make me leave Mike Force.
     Too old. You only one take me on operation.
     Now you don't go.

                   NOONE
     Baap Canh, I'm sorry.

                 BAAP CANH
     No sorry. Time to be free.

Cobb is struck by his words.

                    COBB
     Time to be free...

IN CARTER JAKES' APARTMENT AT NIGHT

Jakes works at a desk. There's a KNOCK. He opens to reveal
MADAME YEN in a white cowled cloak. She lowers the cowl.

                   JAKES
          (surprised)
     Linh...

                 MADAME YEN
     Hello, Carter.

Jakes stares at her.

                 MADAME YEN
     May I come in?

120

He steps back. She enters and glances around.

> MADAME YEN
> I liked your old place better.

> JAKES
> How'd you get through the gate?

> MADAME YEN
> I let the guards check my body for weapons.

> JAKES
> Your body *is* a weapon.

> MADAME YEN
> Are you going to offer me a drink?

Jakes moves to a small bar as she walks the room.

> MADAME YEN
> Same furniture. Still no art.

> JAKES
> I have the vase you gave me.

She picks it up, sets it down. He brings drinks.

> JAKES
> I apologize for Noone. I've taken care of it.

> MADAME YEN
> Have you?

> JAKES
> You're not exactly blameless here.

> MADAME YEN
> A slight miscalculation.

> JAKES
> It should have no effect on other matters.

MADAME YEN

I hope not. We'll see.

She turns gracefully away.

JAKES

That isn't why you came.

MADAME YEN

No.

JAKES

What do you want?

MADAME YEN

It's more what I don't want. I don't want to be in
the heroin business. But to survive...

JAKES

It goes straight to American troops, you know
that. We have an agreement.

MADAME YEN

Yes, but Tong... The profits are much greater. If
something isn't done...

JAKES

What are you asking?

MADAME YEN

He has a large underground heroin factory. Its
loss would bring things back into balance — for
awhile at least.

JAKES

And you know where it is?

MADAME YEN

To the exact meter in the jungle. I also know
which day of the month the stockpile of pure
heroin is greatest.

Jakes says nothing.

                    MADAME YEN
          One phone call from you and a dangerous
          "enemy stronghold" is erased. You win in every
          way. Heroin is destroyed, the balance of opium
          power is restored...

She moves closer.

                    MADAME YEN
          And you would have my deepest... gratitude.

Jakes considers. He is not immune to her ways.

                    JAKES
          I need Tong's support for other things.

                    MADAME YEN
          Why should he suspect you? He'll assume an
          American patrol found what looked like Viet
          Cong and had it bombed. Happens all the time.

                    JAKES
          I get cautious anytime something is too much to
          your advantage.

                    MADAME YEN
          I don't blame you.
                    (touches his cheek)
          I have much to make up for...

IN THE MIKE FORCE COMPOUND AT NIGHT

NOONE and COBB drink alone in deck chairs by the SWIMMING
POOL. The still water is lit by underwater LIGHTS. Sound of
INSECTS.

                    NOONE
          Jesus, Frank. You're like the fucking anchor
          around here.

                    COBB
Yeah, well...

                    NOONE
What about Jakes?

                    COBB
We'll get drunk, he'll tell me how much I'll be
missed, then he'll get somebody else without
skipping a beat. Everybody's expendable.

                    NOONE
How long you got?

                    COBB
Month.

                    NOONE
Maybe it won't be so bad.

                    COBB
Breaking starch every day?

                    NOONE
So retire.

                    COBB
And what? Play golf?

They drink in silence. Two STRIKERS on guard duty wander by the
far end of the pool. They smile at the Americans.

                    COBB
Look at 'em. Sincere, innocent... Only ones here
worth fighting for.

                    NOONE
Seems a bit harsh.

                    COBB
I've been in three wars and I like this one best,
but I've got no fucking clue why we're here.

                    NOONE
          I heard you landed at Normandy.

                    COBB
          Medic. Damn good one. Should've been a
          doctor.

                    NOONE
          World's full of doctors. Opium smugglers, that's
          what's needed.

                    COBB
                (laughs)
          Used to just buy it and dump it in the jungle.
          The point was to make allies of the villagers, not
          be in the business.

                    NOONE
          Then?

                    COBB
          Then Jakes needed the money.

                    NOONE
          Agency going broke?

                    COBB
          Our little enterprise is not an approved budget
          item just yet.

The strikers squat at the pool's edge. Large BUGS, attracted by
underwater lights, flap helplessly on the water's surface.

                    NOONE
          We're on our own?

                    COBB
          If it succeeds, Washington jumps in. That's the
          deal.

                    NOONE
          And if it doesn't?

COBB

I don't even want to think about it.

The strikers laugh like children as they collect live BUGS from the water and stuff them into their mouths.

MONTAGE

The MUSIC is Bob Dylan, "Serve Somebody," as scenes and tableaus from the characters' lives interweave over time:

- Jakes, Cobb and Noone transport guns and opium, and do deals with secret armies in Laos, Cambodia and Vietnam.
- Day after day the North Vietnamese Army pours down the Ho Chi Minh trail with troops, trucks, tanks.
- Noone and Colonel Han talk—even laugh—in Han's cell.
- Madame Yen goes about the business of being an opium queen and bar owner while keeping close watch on Suong Le.
- Y-Bham gains confidence as preparations for revolution speed up. SF soldiers train FULRO troops.
- FULRO troops led by SF soldiers ATTACK NVA CONVOYS on the Ho Chi Minh trail as part of their training.
- Cobb and Baap Canh drink together in the Hilton and become close friends.
- Suong Le attends school and sings half-heartedly at Club Paris. One night, alone in her room, she gazes at the seashell Noone gave her. Later, Madame Yen kisses her bare, reluctant shoulder.
- Noone and Dao talk and sit meditation in the temple garden.
- In the final scene of the montage, Jakes opens his door to reveal Madame Yen in a red cowled cloak. She lowers the cowl. They kiss deeply. END MUSIC.

SERIES OF SHOTS

- Two B-52 BOMBERS drone at 50,000 feet.
- In the JUNGLE below, snakes, monkeys, birds do their thing.
- In Tong's UNDERGROUND FACTORY workers go about the business of making heroin.
- The B-52s' bomb bay doors OPEN.
- In the FACTORY a worker pushes a cart filled with neatly wrapped packages of heroin down a narrow dirt passage to a

large storeroom. The storeroom is nearly full.

- Dozens of BOMBS spew forth from the bellies of the B-52s and plummet in tight lines.
- From above, the BOMBS make tightly clustered puffs as they impact silently on the ground far below.
- In the JUNGLE bombs EXPLODE, sending trees and dirt flying.
- In the FACTORY the ground SHAKES violently. Workers scramble.
- In the JUNGLE bombs EXPLODE, seemingly everywhere at once.
- In the FACTORY dirt rains down on workers. Equipment falls and breaks.
- The WORKER in the storeroom covers his head, trembling. An EXPLOSION erases his existence as the factory takes a direct hit, followed by another and another...
- THE B-52s' bomb bay doors CLOSE...

IN GENERAL TONG'S OFFICE

GENERAL TONG reclines in his leather desk chair. A fay young BARBER dry shaves him with a straight razor.

The RAZOR gently scrapes Tong's cheeks and chin, then continues upwards to lightly shave his forehead, shape the eyebrows. Tong's eyes close. The razor shaves his EYELIDS.

MAJOR CHINH bursts through the door. [*Dialogue in Vietnamese*]

MAJOR CHINH

General!

The startled barber somehow avoids cutting Tong's EYE.

GENERAL TONG

I told you never —

MAJOR CHINH

There's been an incident. The factory...

Tong dismisses the barber, who scurries out.

                    GENERAL TONG
          What about it?

                    MAJOR CHINH
          Destroyed. B-52s.

                    GENERAL TONG
          This month's shipment?

Chinh shakes his head. Tong flies into a rage.

                    GENERAL TONG
          I want to know who did this!

                    MAJOR CHINH
          An American patrol must have—

                    GENERAL TONG
          AAAAH!

Tong PUNCHES a large VASE, shattering it where it stands, then gradually calms, thinking it through.

                    GENERAL TONG
          No. Someone has betrayed us.

His face drips venom.

                    GENERAL TONG
          Find out who and bring him to me.

IN THE HALL OUTSIDE COLONEL HAN'S CELL

NOONE and an MP approach Han's cell. The MP opens the door for Noone.

INSIDE Han is laying on the floor, holding his stomach, blood coming from his mouth. Noone quickly kneels next to him.

                    NOONE
          Han!

                    COLONEL HAN
                     (weakly)
I guess I didn't have as much time as I thought.

                      NOONE
                     (to MP)
He needs a hospital. Now!

IN A MACV HOSPITAL ROOM

HAN lays in one of the beds. An MP sits nearby. NOONE talks with
DR. KEITH HALL in a far corner of the room.

                     DR. HALL
This is way over my head. If the diagnosis he
got in Hanoi is correct—and I think it might
be—there's nothing I can do for him.

                      NOONE
Nothing you can do or nothing anyone can do.

                     DR. HALL
Look, this is extremely rare. Very few surgeons
have any experience with it at all.

                      NOONE
But somebody does?

                     DR. HALL
Nobody in Vietnam.

                      NOONE
Where then?

                     DR. HALL
The only place I know of that's done any
research on it is John's Hopkins. There's a
surgeon there named Petersen who wrote a
journal article on it recently.

IN JAKES' APARTMENT AT NIGHT

JAKES gets out of bed to answer a knock at his door. It's NOONE.

                    JAKES
          It's the middle of the fucking night, for
          Chrissakes.

                    NOONE
          Not in the States. You have a direct line, right?

                    JAKES
          Yeah...?

                    NOONE
          I need to use your phone.

IN NOONE'S PARENT'S' HOME IN THE STATES

Noone's father, WARREN NOONE, answers the phone.

                    WARREN
          Hello.

INTERCUT NOONE/PARENTS

                    NOONE
          Dad. It's Randy.

                    WARREN
          Randy!

LAURA NOONE, Randy's mother hurries into the room.

                    LAURA
          Is he okay?

                    WARREN
          Are you all right?

                    NOONE
          I'm fine.

WARREN
(to Laura)
He's fine.

LAURA
I want to talk to him.

WARREN
Your mother wants to talk to you.

He hands the phone to Laura.

LAURA
Oh baby, every time I watch news footage of the
war I think I see you. I'm so worried.

NOONE
Don't worry, Mom. I'm never on the news.

LAURA
When are you coming home?

NOONE
Not for awhile. I'm sorry, Mom, but I'm in kind
of a hurry. I need to talk to Dad.

LAURA
Okay. Oh baby, I love you so much!

NOONE
I love you, too, Mom.

She hands Warren the phone.

WARREN
Randy, I need to tell you… I need to tell you
how sorry I am. About everything. I fucked up. I
can't stop thinking about it. I fucked up bad. I
know I'll never be able to make up for it, but…
(tears up)
Goddamn it… I know I'll never…

NOONE
(struck with emotion)
Everybody fucks up, Dad. Me worse than most.

WARREN
I'm just so goddamn sorry, son. Please come
home in one piece.

NOONE
(gathering himself)
Dad, I need a favor. A big one.

ACT V: AT AN AIRPORT IN VIETNAM

A commercial airliner touches down.

OUTSIDE HAN'S HOSPITAL ROOM

NOONE sits in a chair in the hall. DR. BRAD PETERSEN and DR.
HALL emerge from Han's room. Noone stands.

NOONE
Dr. Petersen. I'm Randy Noone. Thank you for
coming.

DR. PETERSEN
Thank your father. With what he's paying me I
might retire.

NOONE
Can you help him?

DR. PETERSEN
I won't know until I get in there, but if I see
what I expect to see, I think he has a decent
chance.

IN MADAME YEN'S OFFICE

MADAME YEN stands gazing out a window. KIM is ushered in,
uncertain, puzzled to be there. [*Dialogue in Vietnamese*]

                    MADAME YEN
You are Kim?

                    KIM
           (nods, almost bowing)
Yes, Madame Yen.

                    MADAME YEN
You stay with Sergeant Noone?

                    KIM
Yes...?

Madame Yen walks around her, inspecting the merchandise.

                    MADAME YEN
You're a beautiful girl. You could make a lot of
money working here.

                    KIM
Work for you? I am flattered, but...

                    MADAME YEN
But?

                    KIM
I have been with Randy for awhile now.

                    MADAME YEN
And you think he'll take you to America?

                    KIM
I don't know, I—

                    MADAME YEN
           (calculating)
If he takes anyone it will be my ward, Suong Le.

                    KIM
Pearl? The singer?

MADAME YEN
He told me he was in love with her.

KIM
(heart sinking)
Why would he tell you that?

MADAME YEN
Because we are lovers, your Sergeant Noone and
I. And lovers tell each other everything — don't
they?

KIM
(now really confused)
Why are you doing this? What do you want?

MADAME YEN
A small favor.

Madame Yen hands Kim a thick envelope. Kim looks inside. It's
filled with MONEY.

KIM
I don't understand. What favor?

Madame Yen holds out a small apothecary BOTTLE.

MADAME YEN
Pour this into his drink.

Kim's eyes widen.

MADAME YEN
A few drops should be enough, but better to use
it all.

KIM
I can't, I —

MADAME YEN
You can and you will!

KIM
Why me? You have many people.

MADAME YEN
Because you add the sting of betrayal.

Kim steps back.

MADAME YEN
Refusing me would not be wise. As you say, I
have many people.

Madame Yen takes Kim's HAND and folds her fingers around the
bottle. Kim does not drop it.

ON A WATERFRONT DOCK AT NIGHT

A black car grinds to a stop outside a foreboding warehouse.
GENERAL TONG and his GOONS pile out and go inside.

IN A WATERFRONT WAREHOUSE

MAJOR CHINH and two ARVN soldiers are waiting. QUAN lays
bloody and beaten on the floor. [*Dialogue in Vietnamese*]

MAJOR CHINH
(to Tong)
He refuses to admit anything. But if it was
anyone it had to be him.

Tong bends down. He gently smooth's Quan's hair and strokes his
face as he speaks intimately to him.

GENERAL TONG
You have only one hope of surviving this, my
handsome friend. Do you want to survive this?

Quan nods.

GENERAL TONG
Good. Tell me the truth right now, and I may let
you live — perhaps even pay a reward. But if I

sense one false word, you will die in great pain.
Understand?

                    QUAN
      Yes.

                GENERAL TONG
      Did you tell someone the location of my factory?

                    QUAN
      Yes.

                GENERAL TONG
      Thank you for your honesty. You may yet live
      through this. Who did you tell?

                    QUAN
      Madame Yen.

                GENERAL TONG
      You've done well.

Tong pats Quan's shoulder then stands. Quan looks slightly relieved.

                MAJOR CHINH
                  (to Tong)
      And the bombers?

                GENERAL TONG
      We know who she would ask.

Tong nods to his men. Quan's eyes widen in terror as he is quickly
bound and gagged.

ON A WATERFRONT DOCK AT NIGHT

Goons drag Quan to the edge of the dock. With a nod from Tong,
they rip off Quan's shirt and tie a rope around his chest. Tong pulls a
KNIFE, shows it to the terrified Quan, then DISEMBOWELS him.

Quan is hung from a piling, chest deep in water. The water boils as
FISH FEED on his entrails. His SCREAMS are muffled by his gag.

TONG smiles, then climbs into his car.

IN MADAME YEN'S APARTMENT IN DAYLIGHT

SUONG LE watches from a second story window as MADAME YEN and her BODYGUARDS drive off in a black Mercedes.

IN HER BEDROOM Suong Le takes a SUITCASE from under the bed and opens it. It's already packed. She adds a few things—the crucifix from the wall, the picture of her parents, the seashell Noone gave her—then snaps it closed.

IN A MACV HOSPITAL OPERATING ROOM

DR. PETERSEN operates on Colonel Han, assisted by several Army surgeons. He looks concerned. A nurse wipes his brow.

IN AN ANTIQUE SHOP IN VIETNAM

MADAME YEN is fawned over by the SHOPKEEPER. [*Dialogue in Vietnamese*]

> MADAME YEN
> It has arrived?

> SHOPKEEPER
> More beautiful than I anticipated. Made for a
> French noblewoman.

They look together at a magnificent antique dressing table.

> MADAME YEN
> Exquisite. Have it delivered tomorrow.

> SHOPKEEPER
> For yourself?

> MADAME YEN
> No. A gift for Tet.

ON THE STREET OUTSIDE THE ANTIQUE SHOP

MADAME YEN emerges from the store. Her BODYGUARDS scan the area as they let her in back of the car and climb in front.

From nowhere two Vietnamese HITMEN appear and SHOOT both bodyguards in the head, splattering BLOOD on the windows.

A third hitman drags Madame Yen out, kicking and fighting, as a CAR pulls up. It takes all three of them to stuff her in the back as they pile in after. The car speeds off.

IN COLONEL HAN'S HOSPITAL ROOM

DR. PETERSEN examines HAN, who is recovering, but still groggy. NOONE enters with a small package. He puts a hand on Han's shoulder.

                    NOONE
          How you doing?

Han nods, but is not ready to speak just yet.

                    DR. PETERSEN
                (sincerely pleased)
          He's doing good.

                    NOONE
          Thank you. Thank you.

                    DR. PETERSEN
          Who is he to you?

Noone looks to Han. They share a smile.

                    NOONE
          It's a long story.

Dr. Petersen and Noone shake hands and Petersen leaves. Noone sits on Han's bed and gives him the package, then takes it back and opens it for him. It's a BOOK—a biography of Robert E. Lee.

NOONE

Tomorrow's Tet. Happy birthday.

COLONEL HAN
(weakly)
Thank you.

NOONE

Ordered it awhile back. Of course, Lee was
fighting *against* unification, but any analogy
breaks down if you look too close.

COLONEL HAN

Where will you be tonight?

NOONE
(puzzled by the question)
At Mike Force. Everyone's in for the truce. Why?

COLONEL HAN

My father always told me to avoid crowded
places during Tet.

NOONE

I'd say you're in compliance this year.

COLONEL HAN

It's good advice for anyone, Sergeant.

NOONE

I'll stop by tomorrow.

COLONEL HAN
(beat)
Take care of yourself, Randy.

IN THE NEW MIKE FORCE CLUB AT NIGHT

From the JUKEBOX Janis Joplin wails "Combination of the Two" as
the new teamhouse club is christened on the eve of Tet.

SF SOLDIERS and Vietnamese PROSTITUTES jam the place. The Tet truce has brought everyone in from the field and a big party is in full swing.

A HANDHELD P.O.V. CAMERA winds through the crowd, eavesdropping on candid vignettes and conversations...

KIM AND MAI fast-dance together, looking sexy in mini-skirts and swirling hair. They're good, real good. People watch.

NOONE leans on the new mahogany bar talking to COBB, who has taken up drinking position behind it. MARTY and a couple Vietnamese WOMEN work around Cobb, handing out drinks.

There is a small commotion at the door as COLONEL PULLMAN enters accompanied by Martha Raye, the actress, wearing jungle fatigues and green beret. Here, she goes by MAGGIE.

Maggie draws a crowd and works the room a bit, then spots Cobb and makes her way over. Cobb comes around the bar.

                    MAGGIE
                 (big hug)
          Frank Cobb, you son-of-a-bitch.

                    COBB
          Of all the gin joints in all the jungles, you walk
          into mine.

                    MAGGIE
          We'll always have Saigon.

They laugh. Marty comes over.

                    MAGGIE
          Marty!

They hug across the bar.

                    MARTY
          Vodka rocks?

MAGGIE

Amen.

COBB

You met Randy Noone?

MAGGIE
(liking his looks)

Unh-unh. I'd remember.

NOONE

Good to finally meet you Maggie. Just missed
you a couple of times.

COBB

He's in the bush a lot.

MAGGIE
(double-entendre smile)

I'll bet he is.

Marty brings Maggie's drink.

MARTY

Bob Hope in country?

MAGGIE

Nah, came over on my own.
(pats Cobb's cheek)
I missed my boys.

Colonel Pullman walks up to stand on the other side of Noone.

PULLMAN

What'd you find to drink here? Anything good?

Noone slides him his glass. Pullman sips as Marty watches.

PULLMAN

Macallan?

Marty grins, pulls a bottle of Macallan 18 from under the bar and pours one for Pullman.

                    MARTY
          Had the chance to pick up a couple cases of this
          the other day, sir, but most guys here drink
          bourbon. I was hoping maybe I could put a case
          in your jeep before you leave.

Pullman eyes Noone and Marty, both looking pleased with themselves.

                    PULLMAN
          If you insist.

                    MAGGIE
               (to Cobb)
          Marty will remember.

                    MARTY
          Remember what?

                    MAGGIE
          Was it Pleiku or Qui Nhon where the Liar's Dice
          game got over a thousand bucks?

                    MARTY
          Pleiku.

                    COBB
          Wherever it was, you fucking won, that much I
          remember.

                    MAGGIE
          I'm an actor. Lying's what we do.

Maggie, Cobb, and Marty laugh and catch up in the background as Pullman and Noone talk.

                    PULLMAN
          Everything going all right with Jakes?

NOONE
Yes, sir. More or less. He's either brilliant or
crazy.

PULLMAN
It's not always either-or.

NOONE
Tell the truth, I've had a bad feeling lately. He
convinced Y-Bham to attack NVA units as part
of their training. There's no turning back for
them now. They've got no friends but us.

PULLMAN
We're good friends to have.

NOONE
I hope so.

PULLMAN
I hear you're all buddied up with that NVA
Colonel. Got your father to fly in a surgeon.

NOONE
He'd have died otherwise.

PULLMAN
Lots of NVA die. If I'm not mistaken, it's our job
to kill 'em.

NOONE
You don't approve.

PULLMAN
I'm not second guessing, Noone. I'm sure
you've got your reasons.

NOONE
He's a good man.

PULLMAN
Dropping any hints?

                              NOONE
          Sir?

                           PULLMAN
          Like what the fuck they're up to?

                            NOONE
          I just bring 'em in. Somebody else interrogates.

                           PULLMAN
          Fair enough.

                            NOONE
          He did seem to advise me to stay away from
          crowds for Tet.

                           PULLMAN
                     (grinning at the room)
          Looks like you don't take advice well, son.

                            NOONE
          Does that qualify as a hint?

                           PULLMAN
                     (moving off)
          Who the fuck knows. We'll find out soon
          enough.

The MUSIC segues into Blind Faith, "Can't Find My Way Home."

NOONE'S P.O.V. as he takes in the room — full of people having a
good time. Motion SLOWS almost imperceptibly and it QUIETS
inside as he sees this scene in his life — really SEES it — unfolding with
flawless choreography and subtle perfection...

Across the room, STILES and RENFROW, draped in beautiful
WOMEN, raise their glasses to him as if they, too, feel the moment.

Noone's expression is complex. In it is the joy of being exactly where
he wants to be at the moment, mixed with a recognition of the
heartbreaking pathos and poignancy of human existence. The song
lyrics reflect his mood

144

Come down off your throne and leave your body alone.
Somebody must change.
You are the reason I've been waiting all these years.
Somebody holds the key.
Well, I'm near the end and I just ain't got the time.
I'm wasted and I can't find my way home.

He turns back to the bar and gestures for Marty to refill his drink. He takes a long pull then stares down at his glass.

COBB glances up from his conversation and notices something. He elbows Noone and juts his chin to the exterior door.

COBB

Noone...

Noone turns to see SUONG LE in white *ao dai*, suitcase in hand, looking like a drop-dead gorgeous bride. Heads turn. She looks around and sees NOONE. Their eyes lock. She smiles shyly and walks towards him.

MAGGIE
My God, she's beautiful. Yours?

NOONE

I didn't think so.

SF soldiers stop Suong Le to hit on her.

NOONE
(to Cobb)
You still got your place downtown?

Cobb hands him the key.

COBB
Careful. Curfew's tight tonight.

NOONE

Yes, mother.

Noone turns to go.

                            COBB
          Hang on.

Cobb takes a bottle of champagne from the refrigerator.

                            COBB
          It's her birthday, remember?

Noone moves through the crowd to Suong Le. They only have eyes
for each other. The SF soldiers surrounding her get the picture and
drift off.

                           NOONE
          Let's get out of here.

From across the room, KIM gets the picture, too.

ON A BEACH IN VIETNAM AT NIGHT

A full moon shimmers on dark water. Waves break on pale sand
beneath gently swaying palms...

In the foreground, a JEEP flashes by.

THE JEEP is driven by NOONE. Next to him rides SUONG LE, her
hair swirling sensuously in warm wind.

IN A CITY IN VIETNAM AT NIGHT

NOONE drives slowly past CROWDS celebrating Tet. He turns
down a side street and stops. He and SUONG LE walk through
courtyards to COBB'S HOUSE.

IN COBB'S HOUSE Suong Le watches as Noone lights CANDLES.
They both seem nervous. Noone pops the cork, fills glasses.

                           NOONE
          Happy birthday.

                          SUONG LE
          Happy New Year.

146

Suong Le drinks hers all at once and reacts to the sensation. She puts down her glass, then slowly unbuttons Noone's shirt and slides it from his shoulders. Noone stands motionless as she runs her hands over his skin, barely touching. With erotic restraint, she lingers over each square inch of flesh, then presses her cheek to his chest and closes her eyes...

SERIES OF SHOTS

- In the streets the CELEBRATION continues.
- Outside town a large force of NVA TROOPS are on the move.
- At Mike Force the PARTY rocks on.
- All over the city VC SOLDIERS pull GUNS and MORTARS from hiding places.

IN COBB'S HOUSE

SUONG LE and NOONE lay naked and still in the afterglow. She strokes his cheek and kisses him.

> SUONG LE
> More, please...

IN CARTER JAKES' APARTMENT AT NIGHT

JAKES plays poker with several other AMERICAN MEN in civilian clothes—high ranking government types. Among them is the American AMBASSADOR to Vietnam. Jakes deals a game of stud.

> JAKES
> Possible flush... no help... pair of sevens...
> possible straight... no help.

The players bet their hands. The Ambassador wins this pot.

> JAKES
> Well played, Mister Ambassador.

> AMBASSADOR
> I don't control the cards.

                    JAKES
But some things you do control, or have great
influence over.

                 AMBASSADOR
Your venture has tremendous possibilities,
Carter, but also tremendous risks. Washington
wants to see tangible evidence of success.

                    JAKES
An informal agreement is already in place.

                 AMBASSADOR
There have been a few changes in leadership.
I've been asked to reassure them.

                    JAKES
Look, we have FULRO and all the other
indigenous armies united in one cause. I have a
way to keep the Saigon Air Force out of the air,
and we'll have the enthusiastic support of every
Special Forces swinging dick in country — and all
the indigenous troops they lead.

The Ambassador listens.

                    JAKES
Washington needs to jump in now with full
support. We have the opportunity to win this
fucking war for them!

                 AMBASSADOR
                 (thoughtful)
Very well. I'll recommend in your favor.

Jakes smiles big. The phone rings. Jakes answers.

                    JAKES
Yeah.

IN A WATERFRONT WAREHOUSE AT NIGHT

GENERAL TONG stands with the phone.

> GENERAL TONG
> Mister Jakes. So glad I caught you.

INTERCUT JAKES/TONG

> JAKES
> Tong...

> GENERAL TONG
> You'll be interested to know we're rounding up enemy agents.
> JAKES
> Oh?

> GENERAL TONG
> And executing them.

> JAKES
> Executing?

> GENERAL TONG
> The identities of some are surprising. People you may not have suspected —

> JAKES
> Tong —

> GENERAL TONG
> Or maybe you would —

> JAKES
> Spit it out.

> GENERAL TONG
> There's something I want you to hear, Mister Jakes.

MADAME YEN sits tied to a narrow wooden chair. Tong holds the phone to her mouth.

> MADAME YEN
> Carter?

> JAKES
> Linh!

> MADAME YEN
> I'm sorry —

A GUNSHOT cracks in the phone at Jakes' ear.

> JAKES
> No!

MADAME YEN lays bound to the chair on her side on the floor. The POOL OF BLOOD around her head grows rapidly in size. General Tong holds a SMOKING .45, chrome plated.

> GENERAL TONG
> That's for the airstrike, Mister Jakes.

Jakes is numb.

> GENERAL TONG
> Now if you'll excuse me, I have to bomb a few
> Hmong villages. An uprising is rumored.

The phone goes dead in Jakes' ear.

IN COBB'S HOUSE

NOONE'S EYES pop open in the dark room. In the distance, the sound of GUNFIRE. Then closer, an EXPLOSION. SUONG LE startles awake. Noone jumps up and grabs his pistol.

> NOONE
> Get dressed.

Another EXPLOSION.

NOONE
Hurry!

IN THE MIKE FORCE TEAMHOUSE AT NIGHT

Everyone is half-dressed, hurrying around, talking, shouting, out the door. In the distance, EXPLOSIONS. STILES and several other SF SOLDIERS listen to a field RADIO.

U.S. SOLDIER 1 (O.S.)
(from radio, BG gunfire)
Motherfuckers are everywhere!

U.S. SOLDIER 2 (O.S.)
(from radio)
Roger. We're on the way.

Marty approaches, pulling on clothes.

MARTY
What the fuck's going on?

STILES
Clyde's in town. Sounds like he owns it.

IN THE MIKE FORCE COMPOUND AT NIGHT

SF SOLDIERS and Montagnard STRIKERS man machine guns and mortars on the perimeter. EXPLOSIONS and GUNFIRE rattle the night at intermittent distances.

STILES and RENFROW position their men. MONROE barks out commands. COBB and MARTY arrive at the same mortar station.

MARTY
Where's Noone?

COBB
Must've stayed in town.

MARTY
Pussy's gonna kill him yet.

Marty shouts at some strikers and moves off. BAAP CANH appears, rifle ready. Cobb drops a FLARE ROUND into the tube.

                    BAAP CANH
          We go together, okay?

Cobb looks at him. The FLARE pops high over the landscape, illuminating everything.

                    COBB
          Okay.

IN A CITY IN VIETNAM AT NIGHT

NOONE and SUONG LE leave Cobb's house in faint predawn light and move cautiously through courtyards. They see their JEEP. Noone moves towards it, then spots NVA SOLDIERS. He pulls back out of sight and leads Suong Le a different way.

Pistol ready, Noone and Suong Le sneak around courtyards and alleys, HEARTS POUNDING. Peering around a corner Noone sees NVA soldiers with a machine gun. He leads Suong Le quietly up the outside stairs of a building.

They enter a deserted room and go out a window to the ROOF. Cautiously, they make their way along the rooftops. On the street below, NVA soldiers EXECUTE CIVILIANS.

Suong Le SLIPS. Her foot dislodges a TILE that slides noisily down the roof and BREAKS in the street.

An NVA soldier sees them and FIRES. More NVA soldiers run towards them.

Noone and Suong Le take off running in a tense CHASE over rooftops, NVA soldiers taking potshots at them. They come to a point of no return and JUMP from the roof to a TREE and climb down. Suong Le's face is scratched, drawing BLOOD. Her dress is RIPPED.

They run through back alleys. Turning a corner Noone sees NVA soldiers headed towards them. He ducks just before being seen. The NVA soldiers arrive at the corner and turn in Noone's direction.

From behind several large URNS, Noone and Suong Le watch them pass, not ten feet away.

OUTSIDE THE MIKE FORCE COMPOUND AT SUNRISE

A MOTORCYCLE whines to the gate, NOONE driving, SUONG LE holding tight to his waist. The gate is opened.

IN THE MIKE FORCE TEAMHOUSE

MONROE, RENFROW and STILES shoulder their gear, ready to move out. Noone enters, Suong Le in tow. They both look a mess.

                         MONROE
     Jesus, Noone…

                         NOONE
     What the fuck's happening?

                         MONROE
     Charlie hit every goddamn city in the country.
     We're headed in.

                         NOONE
     I'm coming with you.

Monroe raises an eyebrow at Noone's disheveled unpreparedness.

                         MONROE
     Catch the next one.

                         NOONE
     Give me five minutes.

                         MONROE
     You've got two.

Noone leads Suong Le down the hallway to his room.

IN NOONE'S ROOM

SUONG LE watches silently as NOONE quickly changes into

fatigues, grabs web gear and expertly checks weapons. She has not seen him like this.

> SUONG LE
>
> I'm afraid.

> NOONE
>
> You'll be fine here.

> SUONG LE
>
> For you.

He stops and looks at her.

> SUONG LE
>
> Please come back to me.

Noone pauses a moment then opens a dresser drawer. He hands her an address book.

> NOONE
>
> If anything happens get in touch with my
> parents. They'll get you to the States.

> SUONG LE
>
> I want only you. I am nothing to them.

Noone goes to the armoire and finds an old worn boot. From inside he retrieves a ring box. He opens it and stares at his grandmother's RING. He puts the ring on Suong Le's finger.

> NOONE
>
> You are the wife of their son.

> SUONG LE
> (so many emotions)
> You are my husband forever.

They kiss with deep urgency.

> NOONE
>
> We'll do this better when things settle down.

Noone turns to go. At that moment KIM ENTERS.

                    KIM
          Where you been?!

She sees Suong Le and glares.

                    NOONE
          This is Suong Le.

                    KIM
          Why you bring her here?!

                    NOONE
          She's got nowhere to go.

                    KIM
          You love her?!

Noone looks at Suong Le.

                    NOONE
          Yes. Very much.

Suong Le smiles shyly. Kim unleashes fists on Noone.

                    KIM
          Goddamn you muddafuck!

Noone grabs her wrists.

                    NOONE
          I'll take care of you. I've got money —

                    KIM
          I got money too!

Noone does not have time for this.

                    NOONE
          She stays here! That's it. End of story.
          Everybody's gonna have to just... get along.

Noone grabs his rifle and web gear. He pauses at the door as if to say something, then disappears.

IN THE MIKE FORCE COMPOUND

NOONE runs to catch a troop truck pulling away. Strikers help pull him up into the moving vehicle.

IN NOONE'S ROOM

KIM and SUONG LE stare at each other in silence.

                    KIM
          Do you want something to drink?

IN A U.S. MIITARY COMPOUND IN VIETNAM

A truck full of Hmong STRIKERS pulls through the gate, MARTY driving, COBB shotgun. Soldiers man the walls. The truck stops. Cobb jumps out.

                    MARTY
          Make it fast.

IN JAKES' APARTMENT

JAKES stands over a table spread with papers and maps, an M-16 nearby. Cobb bursts through the door. Jakes grabs his gun, then relaxes.

                    JAKES
          Fucking knock, will ya?

                    COBB
          Have you talked to Y-Bham? They've been
          moving troops across the border for a week.
          He's in perfect position to take advantage of
          this.

                    JAKES
          I told him to stand down. The revolution is on
          hold.

                          COBB

What?! For how long?

                          JAKES

Indefinitely. We'll probably pull the plug.

                          COBB

What the fuck are you talking about?! They
went out on a limb for us! We can't abandon
them now!

Jakes turns on him in sudden anger.

                          JAKES

Did you get the fucking news?! Charlie just
attacked every motherfucking city in the
country at the same time!

                          COBB

It's a gift! He must be desperate. We couldn't
have planned it this good. He's trapped,
nowhere to run. We'll wipe him the fuck out
and the war's over!

                          JAKES

It fucking happened — get it?! And big shot spy
Carter Jakes didn't see it coming. You think
anybody in Washington is gonna play
revolution with me now?!

                          COBB

We need to keep Y-Bham involved so he's a
player when —

In a sudden rage Jakes sweeps the table clean, sending papers flying.

                          JAKES

Goddamn it!!

Cobb studies him.

                    COBB
          What else?

                    JAKES
               (beat)
          Tong killed her.

                    COBB
          Killed who?

                    JAKES
          Linh. Shot her while he had me on the phone.

                    COBB
          Jesus.

BAAP CANH appears at the door.

                    BAAP CANH
          Sergeant Marty say hurry.

Cobb looks at Jakes.

                    JAKES
          We'll talk later. Go.

MONTAGE: MULTIPLE CITIES IN VIETNAM

In an extended sequence, the historic scope and scale of the 1968 TET
OFFENSIVE is conveyed with a mix of B/W DOCUMENTARY
FOOTAGE and SIMULATED documentary footage with compelling
F/X. This is the milieu in which the scripted scenes unfold.

In the final scene of the B/W montage, NOONE and his strikers run
from corner to corner, cover to cover, dodging and returning
automatic weapons fire. In the midst of the scene the B/W film
morphs to color and we are back "live."

IN A CITY IN VIETNAM

STILES, RENFROW, NOONE, and MONROE, each lead groups of
STRIKERS in street fighting and tense house-to-house searches.

STILES and a few strikers enter a building and move cautiously from room to room, HEARTS pounding, BREATH audible. Stiles rounds a corner and draws FIRE. He jumps back and pulls the pin on a GRENADE. He releases the handle and waits a couple seconds before throwing.

After the EXPLOSION he whips around the corner, FIRING full auto. His footfalls echo as he approaches the body of the NVA soldier he killed. He looks at it without expression.

RENFROW exchanges fire with an NVA soldier in an alley. The NVA soldier runs away. Renfrow has a clear shot at his back but doesn't pull the trigger. He lowers his rifle.

MONROE leads his strikers through alleys, in and out of houses. He disappears into a light green house and after a few seconds there is an EXPLOSION. SMOKE pours from the doorway.

MACHINE GUNS nearby open up on the strikers outside, driving them back. They return fire but are badly outgunned. They back away firing in retreat.

INSIDE CLUB PARIS

PROSTITUTES in simple clothes huddle nervously in conversation. The BARTENDER absently polishes glasses behind the bar. Armed HOODS peer out windows. In Madame Yen's absence, CADEO has taken charge.

OUTSIDE CLUB PARIS

VC SOLDIERS move into position across from the club. They open fire and a blazing BATTLE ensues as the HOODS return fire.

CLUB PARIS IS DESTROYED by explosions and gunfire.

When the hoods are all dead, the VC flood inside. Surviving prostitutes huddle in fear. When it is secure, a self-righteous VC OFFICER strides in. He has waited a long time to purge his country of places like this.

He orders the prostitutes dragged outside. At the first sound of
SCREAMS, the BARTENDER rises from behind the bar and starts
shooting. He takes a couple VC with him before being RIPPED
APART by bullets.

OUTSIDE, as the VC officer barks orders, the prostitutes' hands are
tied. Long ROPES are looped around their NECKS and the other
ends thrown over upper balcony rails. The women are hoisted high
to DANGLE AND KICK until dead.

CHAU, Cobb's friend with the beauty mark, is among them.

IN A CITY IN VIETNAM

COBB and MARTY lead strikers through town, looking for enemy.
It's tense, heart-pounding work.

ON A BALCONY, two NVA SOLDIERS man a rocket launcher. A
third aims his sniper rifle and fires.

MARTY IS HIT in the back and goes down.

                          COBB
          Marty!

Cobb drags him into an alley. Marty's shirt is covered with blood.
His open eyes see nothing. His breath rattles.

                          COBB
          Medic!

A striker appears with a medical kit. Cobb tears open Marty's shirt to
reveal a gaping EXIT WOUND.

                          COBB
          Sweet Jesus.

Cobb presses bandages against it. Marty's eyes loose focus.

                          COBB
          Marty! Goddamn it! Marty!

Cobb shoots him with epinephrine, works desperately to save him. Marty's eyes roll back. The light goes out.

An AMERICAN TANK rumbles by on the street.

ON A BALCONY an NVA soldier aims his ROCKET LAUNCHER.

NVA SOLDIER'S P.O.V. through the sights. The tank is in the crosshairs. The ROCKET FIRES and heads towards it.

THE TANK takes an EXPLOSIVE HIT and stops in its tracks. BLACK SMOKE pours from the hatch. A U.S. SOLDIER struggles out, his body covered in thick FLAMES. He falls heavily to the street, ENVELOPED IN FIRE.

Cobb starts towards him. SNIPER FIRE hits near and sends him back into the alley.

                         COBB
                  (to his strikers)
          This way!

Cobb leads his strikers through courtyards and alleys, then cautiously up the stairs of a building. On the upper floor he moves to a window and looks out, getting the lay of the land. He tries several more windows. Finally he sees them.

On a nearby balcony is the NVA SNIPER and the two NVA with the rocket launcher.

Cobb supports his M-16 on the window sill. After a long moment he fires single SHOTS in rapid succession. The three NVA soldiers are hit repeatedly. Cobb continues to shoot into their motionless bodies until his clip is empty.

IN ANOTHER PART OF THE CITY

NOONE kneels at the corner of a building and fires up the street. He and his strikers run and flatten against a wall. After a moment, they run up the street and into a courtyard. They move cautiously through it, hearts pounding. They emerge onto another street.

Across the street, JIENG, a Hmong striker, waves urgently. Noone and his men move quickly across to him. A dozen other strikers are with him, some wounded. A striker medic tends them.

> JIENG
> Captain, he hurt. Maybe dead.

> NOONE
> Where?

Jieng points vaguely. Noone gets on the radio and calls for an ambulance, then turns to Jieng.

> NOONE
> Take me.

Noone picks some strikers to come with him, then points to one of the remaining men.

> NOONE
> (in Rhade)
> When the truck comes get the wounded out and
> hold this position. We'll be back with the
> Captain.

NOONE and his STRIKERS move out. Forced to avoid the streets now, they make their way through alleys and courtyards, expecting to be ambushed at any second. They come to a huge black SEWAGE POND covered with floating garbage and dead rats. By hugging close to a building they are able to wade a shallow edge.

On the other side they continue cautiously through winding outdoor passageways until they come to a light green building. Jieng nods to Noone. They creep up to it and cautiously go inside.

MONROE lays on his back in a pool of blood. His face is torn, his stomach a mess. Noone kneels next to him and checks his pulse at the neck. Monroe's EYES POP OPEN, startling Noone.

                              NOONE
               It's okay. We got you.
                         (to strikers, in Rhade)
               Find something to carry him on.

Noone gives Monroe morphine and tends to his wounds as best he
can. The strikers show up with a LADDER.

                              NOONE
               Let's go.

Monroe moans as he's laid on the ladder. Two strikers pick it up.

OUTSIDE, Noone leads them back the way they came. He sees the
black SEWAGE POND ahead and motions the strikers to stop. They
put down the ladder while Noone scouts a way around it. He hurries
down an alley to the open street. It seems clear.

Suddenly, MACHINE GUN FIRE sends him diving. He runs back.

                              NOONE
                          (in Rhade)
               Get him up! Get him up!

The strikers follow Noone into the SEWAGE POND — the only way
out. Those carrying the ladder are forced to wade farther out into the
pond. Monroe's weight SINKS them into the muck.

NOONE JUMPS IN and grabs the LADDER just as a striker starts to
go under. There is a scramble and it looks for a moment as if Monroe
will get dumped, but they get him safely to the other side.

IN AN ARVN MILITARY COMPOUND

JAKES pulls up to the gate in a truck and is let through. ARVN
soldiers on full alert man the walls.

IN GENERAL TONG'S STAFF OFFICES

ARVN staff, outfitted for battle, scurry from one task to another.
Jakes approaches MAJOR CHINH, who is shocked to see him.

                         JAKES
Tong in?

                         MAJOR CHINH
He's busy.

                         JAKES
Everybody's busy. Tell him I'm here.

IN GENERAL TONG'S OFFICE

TONG talks heated strategy with other ARVN officers as the intercom BUZZES. [*Dialogue in Vietnamese*]

                         GENERAL TONG
                    (answering intercom)
What?!

                         MAJOR CHINH
                    (from intercom)
Jakes is here.

Amazed, Tong considers.

                         GENERAL TONG
Make sure he's not armed.

The door opens, Jakes enters. He and Tong stare at each other.

                         GENERAL TONG
We're rather busy, Mister Jakes. Seems we're
under attack.

                         JAKES
This won't take long.

Jakes looks at the others. Tong considers, then barks some general instructions and sends the officers out, leaving he and Jakes alone. Jakes walks the room, choosing his words.

                         JAKES
          I was angry at first, of course... But as a business
          decision, I understand your actions.

Tong is skeptical.

                         JAKES
          I was wrong to... interrupt your operations.

Tong relaxes slightly.

                         JAKES
          With Madame Yen gone, it's even more
          important you and I have a good relationship.

                    GENERAL TONG
          The opium continues to grow. There is a lot of
          money to be made.

                         JAKES
          Too much to be squandered on revenge.

                    GENERAL TONG
          Perhaps this unpleasantness will turn out for the
          best.

In his pacing of the room Jakes has maneuvered himself close to a
wall display of antique SWORDS. Tong stands nearby.

                         JAKES
          What's important is the future.

                    GENERAL TONG
          Yes, the future.

Jakes extends his hand. Tong takes it.

                         JAKES
          Cuban?

Tong smiles and turns for the box. In a flash Jakes rips a Japanese SWORD from the wall. Tong reacts to the SOUND, but too late. He takes a glancing BLOW to the head and staggers.

Jakes swings again. Tong weakly raises his arm to fend off the sword. It cuts through bone like butter. Tong's ARM FALLS to the floor.

Tong reels, mouth agape. Jakes unleashes a HOME-RUN SWING. The sword cuts halfway through Tong's chest. They freeze, eyes locked. Jakes lets go. Tong falls, eyes wide and unbelieving.

Sudden POUNDING on the door.

                         MAJOR CHINH
          General?!

Jakes grabs the chrome-plated .45 from Tong's holster as MAJOR CHINH bursts through the door, gun in hand. Jakes SHOOTS him twice in the chest, sending him backwards.

Jakes runs to the balcony — second floor. He flips over the railing to the ground. From the office above, SHOUTS. Jakes runs limping to his TRUCK and cranks it.

From Tong's balcony OFFICERS SHOUT to soldiers below. Soldiers FIRE on the truck as Jakes floors it. BULLETS RIP the cab, shattering the windshield. Jakes is HIT.

Guards jump clear as Jakes PLOWS THROUGH the gate, metal flying. Soldiers FIRE at the receding truck. Officers SHOUT. Soldiers jump in TRUCKS and take off through the gate after Jakes.

DOWN THE STREET Jakes throws his truck into neutral, JUMPS and rolls. He looks up to see the truck CRASH into the side of a building, then limps into an alley and disappears.

ARVN trucks and jeeps arrive at the scene of the crash. Jakes' crumpled truck EXPLODES INTO FLAMES.

IN A CITY IN VIETNAM

Two ambulance medics work on MONROE as NOONE watches.

                              NOONE
What's the word?

                       AMBULANCE MEDIC
He'll make it. But not by much.

The medics lift MONROE'S stretcher to put him in the truck. Monroe
weakly raises his hand towards Noone. Noone takes it. They look
into each other's eyes.

                              NOONE
I know…

The medics slide Monroe's stretcher into the truck, as Noone and
STILES help wounded STRIKERS into the truck. It drives off.

Noone pulls a soggy pack of cigarettes from his pocket and tosses it.
RENFROW hands him a smoke and flicks open his lighter.

                             RENFROW
Nice cologne.

                              NOONE
Thanks.

                              STILES
We can each take some of Monroe's platoon. I
need the men anyway. Lost four this morning
over by some temple.

                              NOONE
Buddhist? Few blocks east?

                              STILES
Yeah. Charlie's thick as shit in there.

                              NOONE
                           (considers)
How about we head back that way?

                              STILES
Fine with me.

                              RENFROW.
          Let's do it.

NOONE, STILES, RENFROW and their strikers fight their way
through streets and back alleys, taking and returning heavy fire. Both
sides take casualties. Finally, NOONE sees the TEMPLE and makes a
break for it. MACHINE GUN FIRE sends him diving.

AN NVA SOLDIER drops a MORTAR ROUND into the tube.

NOONE approaches the TEMPLE at a run. GUNFIRE rattles after
him. He takes cover and fires at random, then starts running again. A
mortar round EXPLODES in the street behind him as he charges into
the temple.

INSIDE THE BUDDHIST TEMPLE

NOONE sees the temple has been hit hard. Much of it is rubble. He
runs from room to room.

IN THE TEMPLE COURTYARD

DAO sits lotus position, eyes closed. The sound of a mortar
EXPLODING outside the wall does not faze him. NOONE bursts into
the courtyard.

                              NOONE
          Dao!

Dao opens his eyes and smiles.

                              NOONE
          We have to go.

A mortar round EXPLODES on the temple ROOF!

                              NOONE
          Now!

                              DAO
          My place is here.

Noone grabs Dao by the arm. Their eyes lock.

                          DAO
                    (wise whisper)
          Let go...

Noone's eyes widen and his expression suddenly softens. He takes a step backwards, almost trancelike, then another.

A mortar round EXPLODES — RIGHT BEHIND DAO!

NOONE'S P.O.V. as in SLOW MOTION the explosion HALOES Dao with a blinding backlight. Color adjust until he's a dark silhouette — a BUDDHA STATUE against a background of RAGING ORANGE.

NOONE is lifted into the air and seemingly frozen as motion almost stops. SHRAPNEL moves towards him at extremely slow speeds, slowly tearing his fatigues and entering his flesh.

His FACE is brilliantly lit by the explosion and an INNER LIGHT.

NOONE'S P.O.V. as a piece of SHRAPNEL heads for the space between his eyes. Inside the shrapnel a VISION forms. It grows to fill the screen.

The P.O.V. ANGLE enters the vision and bursts into an OTHERWORLDLY LANDSCAPE. It soars through an endless landscape of mounds and cliffs, bottomless pits and soaring peaks. Viewed close, the surfaces are covered with tiny MOVEMENT.

CLOSER, the movement appears to be INSECTS, tightly packed like bees in a hive.

CLOSER STILL, it is seen to be PEOPLE, billions of billions — everyone who ever lived or will.

THE P.O.V. ANGLE swoops and dives to find the tiny figure of NOONE among the billions.

The figure of Noone looks up and stares into the P.O.V. ANGLE with wonder, awe, recognition — then ecstatic, unbridled JOY.

The head of the figure becomes a FIERY SUN.

The P.O.V. ANGLE ENTERS THE FIRE. Now there is only CLEAR LIGHT and the sensation of incredible SPEED, until we burst through to the dark side of light, to the infinite CLEAR BLACK of the timeless Void...

EPILOGUE: ON BLACK

> BAAP CANH (V.O.)
> (in Rhade, subtitles)
> Fear nothing. Do not flee...
> May your soul not be frightened into slavery...

CLOSE ON BAAP CANH'S FACE

> BAAP CANH
> May your soul not be frightened into deafness...

PULL BACK to reveal he squats before a BODY surrounded by small ceremonial fires and an array of shamanic objects.

> BAAP CANH
> May your soul not be frightened into a swift
> return...

PULL FURTHER BACK to reveal we are in a Hmong village. It is the body of an old HMONG MAN receiving funeral rites.

> BAAP CANH
> Remain close to the rainbow...
> Be at peace in the underworld.

NEARBY, under a thatched-roof shelter, FRANK COBB holds sick call for villagers. He wears native black pajamas. His long hair is tied back in a ponytail.

IN A BAR IN A MIDDLE EASTERN CITY AT NIGHT

CARTER JAKES, full beard, drinks alone at a corner table. It's a small place with the smoky ambiance of the Casbah. The PATRONS should not be trusted.

Two unsavory ARAB MEN enter and look around. They spot Jakes and head for his table.

Behind the bar, an ARAB WOMAN, forties, her exotic beauty diminished only slightly by age, tends bar. She observes Jakes' table with interest.

Jakes and the two men talk briefly. Envelopes are exchanged and quickly pocketed. The men leave. Jakes and the bartender exchange smiles. They know each other well.

IN A HOUSE IN HANOI, VIETNAM

COLONEL HAN, in civilian clothes, plays with his four-year old grandson. His wife and daughter sit laughing and talking nearby.

IN A RUSTIC JUNGLE PRISON IN VIETNAM

GENERAL Y-BHAM ENOUL squats on the dirt floor of his cell. His face shows the strain of torture. TWO NVA SOLDIERS enter and tie his hands. He is led past other cells, HMONG MEN peering out.

OUTSIDE THE JUNGLE PRISON

General Y-Bham Enoul is stood against a tree in front of a FIRING SQUAD. An NVA OFFICER approaches with a blindfold.

General Y-Bham Enoul's P.O.V. as the blindfold is applied. In DARKNESS his intimate BREATH dominates other sounds.

NVA OFFICER (O.S.)
(in Vietnamese)

Ready... Fire.

SHOTS crack. Dark silence.

DISSOLVE TO:

EXTREME CLOSE-UP of the back of a DARK JACKET.

The DARKNESS MOVES ASIDE as the wearer of the jacket opens a DOOR. Behind the door is a narrow curved tunnel.

After a moment, PEOPLE approach with carry-on luggage. We are...

AT AN ARRIVAL GATE IN A MAJOR U.S. AIRPORT

An AIRLINE EMPLOYEE in dark uniform holds the gate door as passengers emerge into the terminal.

Among those waiting are WARREN and LAURA NOONE. They watch the passengers arrive with nervous anticipation. The stream of people through the gate slows, then stops. They look at each other and at the vacant gate door.

Then SUONG LE emerges, sees them wave, and approaches. At her side is BRANDY NOONE, a four-year old Amerasian girl whose FACE lights the world. She has Noone's eyes.

Laura's hand goes to her mouth as emotion floods.

> SUONG LE
> (to her daughter)
> Brandy, these are your grandparents.

Laura stoops to the child's level. Brandy looks to her mother, who nods. Brandy embraces her grandmother. Warren fights emotion.

> WARREN
> You should have written sooner.

> SUONG LE
> We did not want to be a bother.

> LAURA
> (holding Brandy tight)
> Oh baby...

OUTSIDE THE AIRPORT AT NIGHT

A limousine awaits as they emerge from the terminal. Warren carries his granddaughter. His chauffeur smiles at the scene as he holds the door for everyone.

INSIDE THE LIMOUSINE

LAURA and SUONG LE ride on the back seat, reminding us of a similar shot in the opening sequence with Suong Le and Madame Yen. On the seat facing them, WARREN plays with BRANDY.

MUSIC fades up—a moving new arrangement of Deep Forest's "Sweet Lullaby," ("Rorogwela") sung by the voice of Suong Le. It begins *a cappella*, then more voices and instruments are added.

The translated lyrics are displayed as SUBTITLES as she sings:

> *Little child, little child, hush now, hush now...*
> *Even though you keep crying*
> *I will carry you.*
> *Your father has gone to the afterlife.*
> *From the island of the dead he watches over us.*
> *Protect the elders. Protect the orphans.*

SUONG LE looks out her window at the city. REFLECTIONS drift across her window and face...

> *Little child, little child, hush now, hush now...*
> *Even though you keep crying*
> *I will hold you.*
> *From the island he cares for us like royalty,*
> *with all the wisdom of that garden.*
> *Protect the elders. Protect the orphans.*

ON THE STREETS people of every description go about their lives. Every FACE holds a story...

PULL BACK to a long shot of DOWNTOWN as cars and people flow to the horizon in every direction. The SONG adds a chorus of voices...

PULL FURTHER BACK until we see the whole CITY FROM ABOVE, a crystalline jewel of lights...

Then back further still to a LANDSCAPE of lighted cities, networked like NEURONS... The CHORUS of voices builds to thousands it seems...

Continuing back, the landscape of neurons gradually morphs into the FRACTAL DARKNESS OF INFINITY...

The music continues under CREDITS.

The song is hypnotic...

FADE OUT

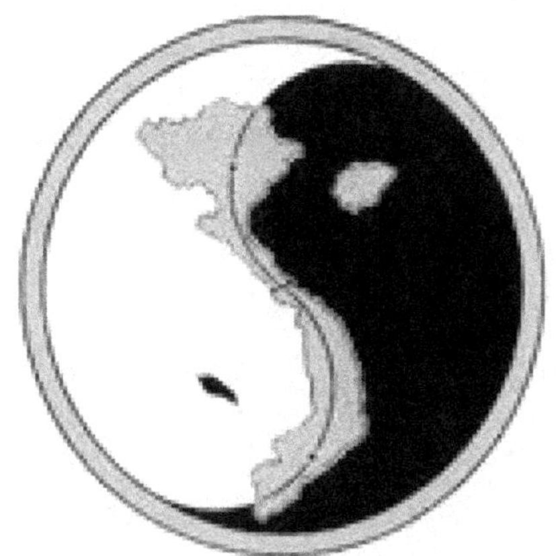

MIKE FORCE

II CORPS MIKE FORCE
BIG PARTYS CLUB
PLEIKU VIETNAM

Maggie at Big Marty's Club

TERRY
AND THE PIRATES
by
MILTON CANIFF
enter the
DRAGON LADY

CO

HAI-BIEN
HAI BIEN
VIEN UON TOC
Huỳnh Mai
69 - PHAM-NGU-LAO
KỲ-NGHỆ LẠNH
71 - PHAM - NGU
UON TOC
S.0235

Full Page of Moon Photos
RACING
Los Angeles Times
FINAL
VIET CRISIS GROWS
Dies In Viet
1st Photos of Viet Mass
THE PLAIN DEALER
THE VIET-CONG
TET OFFENSIVE
1968
Excl
The New York Times
WESTMORELAND REQUESTS
206,000 MORE MEN, STIRRED
DEBATE IN ADMINISTRATION
XTRA
Los Angeles Times
FINAL
De-escala
The Globe and Mail
CANADA LIFE
Diplomat kills fighter
Viet Cong suicide mission
wiped out at U.S. Embassy
Constitution
Parts of building
held for 6 hours
LIFE
New frenzy in the war
Vietcong terrorize the cities
SUICIDE RAID ON
THE EMBASSY
Vietnam Casual
WASHINGTON (S&S) — The
Defense Department has an-
nounced the following casualties
in connection with the conflict in
Vietnam.
KILLED IN ACTION
Chicago Tribune
FINAL
RECAPTURE U.S. EMBASSY
GIs Land in Copters on Saigon Roof,
Wipe Out Viet Cong in 6-Hour Battle
REDS BLAST HOLE IN
WALL TO GAIN ENTRY
VC HIT SAIGON
Reds Invade Embassy, Air Base
STAR STRIPES

Y-Bham Enoul

PEARL OF THE ORIENT

Cast
In Order of Appearance

Old Monk
Madame Yen
Suong Le
Dao
Randy Noone
Lyle Decker
Baap Canh
Reeby
Carter Jakes
Frank Cobb
General Tong
Colonel Han
NVA Captain
NVA Sergeant
Kim
Paul Renfrow
Dan Stiles
Mai
Captain Steve Monroe
Big Marty
Colonel John Pullman
Chau
Bartender
General Y-Bham Enoul
Y-Gar
Cadeo
Major Chinh
Quan
Dr. Hall
Warren Noone
Laura Noone
Dr. Petersen
Maggie
American Ambassador
Brandy Noone

PEARL OF THE ORIENT

Sound Track

"God Bless the Child" — Billie Holliday

"The Wind Cries Mary" — Jimi Hendrix

"La Vie en Rose" — voice of Suong Le (channeling Edith Piaf)

"Don't Explain" — voice of Suong Le (channeling Billie Holliday)

"Begin the Beguine" — voice of Suong Le

"Crazy" — Patsy Cline

"Serve Somebody" — Bob Dylan

"Combination of the Two" — Big Brother and the Holding Company

"Can't Find My Way Home" — Blind Faith

"Rorogwela" — voice of Suong Le (channeling Afunakwa)